CRIT

"A brilliant second outing . . . a top-notch mystery,
engaging throughout and quite moving at the end."
—*Publishers Weekly* **(starred review)**

"Original . . . a wonderful discovery."
—*Denver Post*

"Carter has an incredibly hot property here: Nanette
Hayes may be the most charismatic crime fiction hero-
ine to appear in the last decade. . . . Throw in Carter's
jazz history–drenched plot and her terrific feel for incor-
porating setting into the action, and you have a
superbly entertaining novel."
—*Booklist* **(starred review)**

"Treat yourself to a look and a listen. . . . You'll love Nan."
—*Hartford Courant*

"A fun book. . . . Nanette is charming . . . with perfect
taste, and we'll gladly follow her anywhere."
—*Denver Rocky Mountain News*

"Briskly written . . . successful."
—*London Free Press*

more . . .

"Four stars! As sexy, smooth, and rhythmic as a fine jazz combo, COQ AU VIN is a gem of a novel. . . . Touches of noir highlight the compelling story line, and music lovers will find the many references to music and musicians an added bonus."
—**Romantic Times**

"Full of soul."
—**Hackensack Record** (NJ)

"You can smell the food, savor walking the streets, and breathe in the essence of the City of Lights. . . . An enjoyable story with a rich assortment of characters."
—**I Love a Mystery**

. . . AND CHARLOTTE CARTER'S PREVIOUS NOVEL *RHODE ISLAND RED*

"Wholly delightful . . . the year's freshest crime debut."
—**GQ** magazine

"Sharp, funny, and beautifully underscored with jazzy prose riffs. . . . Welcome to this year's most original fictional detective."
—**Good Housekeeping**

"Gritty."
—**Kirkus Reviews**

Also by Charlotte Carter

Rhode Island Red
Drumsticks

CHARLOTTE CARTER

Coq au Vin

WARNER BOOKS

A Time Warner Company

The events and characters in this book are fictitious. Certain real locations and actual historical figures are mentioned, but all other characters and the events described in the book are totally imaginary.

WARNER BOOKS EDITION

Cover design by Rachel McClain
Cover illustration by Paul Rogers

Warner Books, Inc.
1271 Avenue of the Americas
New York, NY 10020

Visit our Web site at
www.twbookmark.com

 A Time Warner Company

Printed in the United States of America

Originally published in hardcover by The Mysterious Press
First Paperback Printing: February 2000

10 9 8 7 6 5 4 3 2 1

For Drew Gangolf

Acknowledgments

For friendship and support offered, for the examples they set and for the luck they have brought me, I wish to thank Lisa Carlson, Larry Eidelberg, Susanna Einstein, Estelle Gerard, Margo Jefferson, Martha Jones, Patricia Spears Jones, Frank King, Bill Kushner, Bernadette Mayer, Suzanne McConnell, Mark McCormick, Jackie McQueen, Shirley Sarris, Laurie Stone, Serpent's Tail, Lynne Tillman, Gary Woodard.

CHAPTER 1

Travelin' Light

Damn, I was tired. My saxophone seemed to weigh more than I did.

I had awakened early that morning and immediately commenced to fill the day with activity—some of it necessary but most of it far from pressing.

I played for a time midtown, a little north of the theater district; made some nice money. That wasn't my usual stomping ground. I had picked the corner almost at random. I don't know why I did so well. Maybe the people had spring fever, hormones working, calling out for love songs. In fact the first song I played was "Spring Fever." When you play on the street, you never know why you're a hit or a bust. Is it the mood of the crowd? Is it you? Is it the time of day or the time of year? Anyway, you do the gig and put your money in your belt and move on.

Next, I power-walked up to Riverside Park and played there for a while; did my two hours volunteer work at the soup kitchen on Amsterdam; bought coffee beans at Zabar's; took the IRT downtown; bought a new reed for the sax on Bleecker Street; picked up some paint samples at the hardware store; then played again on lower Park Avenue, closer to my own neighborhood.

Makes me sound like a real flamer, doesn't it? A go-getter, a busy bee. Not true. I'm lazy as hell.

What I was doing was trying to outrun my thoughts. That's what all that busy work was about.

Over dinner the previous night, the b.f. (the shit-head's name is Griffin) had announced, number one, he wouldn't be spending the night at my place because he had other plans, and number two, he had other plans . . . period.

I should have known something was up when he said to meet him at the little Belgian café I like in the Village—the other side of town from my place. He hated the food there, but it was convenient for his subway ride home.

This kind of thing has happened to me before. The relationship is at some critical point—or maybe not; maybe it's simply that a certain amount of time has passed and I'm re-evaluating it. I meet his family. Mom wants to know if this is "the real thing." I'm asking myself constantly, Is the sex really that good? Should I stay in or should I get out?

And then, a couple of weeks later, before I come to a final decision, he splits.

What's with that?

I always seem to end up asking myself that question. What is with that?

I didn't spend the night crying or anything. I merely

came in and stripped out of my clothes and snapped on the radio and finished whatever brown liquor I had in the cabinet. Temper tantrum aside, breaking the porcelain planter in the living-room window had been more of an accident than anything else.

Sleep was a long time coming. Yes, I had decided about two A.M., the sex *had* been *that* good. And when I awoke in the morning, I just started moving like this— manic.

Now I was exhausted. I packed up my sax and started the short walk to my apartment near Gramercy Park.

Our homeless guy was back. It had been so long since anybody had seen him on the block, we all figured he was dead. But here he was again, in a neck brace, evil as ever, begging for dollars and cussing at anybody with the nerve to give him coins. "Why don't you comb your hair?" he called after me when I stuffed a single into his cup.

I made a quick run to the supermarket and then into the benighted little corner liquor store where a white wine from Chile is the high-end stuff.

I had poured myself a glass, turned on the radio, and read through the mail before I remembered to check the answering machine.

"Nanette, it's me. About tonight. You're still coming over to eat, aren't you? Because I've got something to tell you. It's . . . I'm . . . Well, I'll tell you when you get here. I'm going out now to pick us up some food at Penzler's. You still eat pork, don't you, baby?"

Mom!

Oh shit.

I had forgotten. Two weeks ago I had said maybe we'd

have dinner—I walked over to the kitchen calendar—tonight.

I was in no mood to see anybody tonight, let alone Mom, for whom I'd have to put on an act—make out that things were fine between me and Griffin, and that my fabulous—and utterly fictitious—part-time job teaching French at NYU was going great. I'd have to be careful never to mention the sax or my street friends or anything remotely connected to my career as an itinerant musician on the streets of Manhattan. She might have been able to handle it if she ever found out that the teaching job was a lie (I was getting steady translation work, at least). But she would have gone absolutely crazy if she knew I blew sax on the street corners with an old fedora turned up to catch the cash. *And* I'd have to haul my ass on the F train out to Queens.

Well, I just wasn't going to make it. Not with all these papers to grade. Not with this pneumonia, cough cough. Not tonight. Tomorrow maybe, but not tonight.

I've got something to tell you.

I turned that gossipy, girlish phrase over in my mind. What was there about that locution that troubled me so? It didn't sound like Mrs. Hayes, that's what. It just did not sound right. And, come to think of it, there was a bit of a quaver in her voice, too.

Oh, God. She's sick. Heart. Cancer.

I rushed to the wall phone and dialed her number. No answer.

I threw my jacket on and locked up.

Halfway to the subway, I realized I was probably being crazy. There were only about three million other reasons my mother might have had to sound worried. Maybe it really was something about her health, but that didn't have to mean that death was knocking on the door.

So why hadn't she answered the phone? She was probably still at Penzler's—Elmhurst's answer to Dean and Deluca—inspecting the barbecued chickens and braised pork chops and waiting on line for a pound of potato salad. Or out in the backyard. Or over at the Bedlows' house, picking up one of Harriet's cobblers for our dessert.

By then I was at Sixth Avenue. I turned downtown instead of north to the Twenty-third Street station. It was a spur-of-the-moment thing. I had suddenly decided I needed a drink before heading out there, and I needed a little reassuring from the one person whose level head and unfailing equilibrium I could always depend on: my one and only homegirl, Aubrey Davis. Who works as a topless dancer.

We knew early on, at about age nine, that I was the whiz at sight-reading music, inventing lies more believable than the truth, and forging my mother's signature. "Very bright, but a bit unfocused," one of my teachers had told Daddy on parents' night.

Aubrey, however, was the one to call when you wanted to see some dancing. She struggled mightily to teach me one or two moves. But it was no good. I could work the shoulders, and I could usually work the hips too—just not at the same time. To this day, when I hit the dance floor I look like a holdup man who realizes too late that his victim is carrying a taser. By the time we were fourteen we'd both thrown in the towel on my dancing career.

It was about that time, on a summer day, that Aubrey's mother abandoned her. She went off to play cards with

some people and just never came back. In school, I was
the brightest star in the heavens, but Aubrey, when she
deigned to join us, was the butt of the kids' pitiless taunt-
ing—about her clothes, about her poverty, about her
mother, and in time, about her morals. The oddsmakers
wouldn't have laid ten cents on Aubrey's chances of getting through life in one piece. They'd have lost. She is a
genius at taking care of herself. And my girl never wastes
a second looking backward.

Anyway, Aubrey is now one of the bigger draws at
Caesar's Go Go Emporium, which is exactly the kind of
place it sounds like, tied however circuitously to the mob
and located in that one dirty corner of Tribeca where
Robert De Niro has not yet bankrolled any emigre restau-
rateurs.

She performs topless, like I said, and what she wears
over the nasty bits is barely worthy of the term "panties."
Between weekly pay and tips she makes a pretty impressive salary, only a fraction of which gets declared to the
tax folks. I don't know all the details, but I believe
Aubrey has an enviable little portfolio going, thanks to
one of her Wall Street admirers. I can always hit her up
for money, but I made a vow long ago never to do so unless I was starving. See, if you ask her for a couple of
hundred, the next thing you know, she's putting down a
deposit on a new co-op for you. She is that generous. She
is also a great beauty, and I love her madly. So does my
mother, who took turns with the other grown-ups in the
neighborhood in trying to raise her.

I heard the pounding bass line from halfway up the
block. Caesar's. I hate that fucking place. I hate the white
men in their middle-management ties who come in for

their fix of watery scotch and flaccid titties. I hate the rainbow coalition of construction worker types in their Knicks T-shirts drinking Coors and spending their paychecks on blow jobs. And I've got zero patience with all of them. Not Aubrey, though. She understands men—all kinds of men. And boy, do they love her and her Kraft caramel thighs and her cascades of straightened hair and her voice like warm apple butter.

It is little wonder that Aubrey became a superstar, if you will, at Caesar's. A lot of the other dancers are distracted college girls who'd rather shake their ass in a dive than work behind a cosmetics counter somewhere, or they're skanks strung out on crack and pills. But Aubrey, who isn't even much of a drinker, is focused, engaged, thoroughly there when she's dancing. She has a fierce kind of dedication to her work, and the guys seem to pick up on that immediately. It is the damnedest thing, but they appear to respect her.

There was no one on stage when I walked into the darkened room. The girls were taking a break. I walked double time through the crowd of horny men, and had almost made it back to the dressing rooms when I heard a male voice call my name. My whole body stiffened for a few seconds. I kept walking, but the voice rang out again: "Hey, Nan!"

I stopped and turned then. I couldn't believe that any man who actually knew me would not only be hanging in a place like this but would actually want me to *see* him in here.

To my relief, it was only Justin, the club manager. He was standing at the end of the bar, his signature drink, dark rum and tonic, in one hand and one of those preposterously long thin cigarettes in the other. Justin, self-described as "white trash out of Elko, Indiana," is Aubrey's most ardent fan. Of course, his admiration for her has no sexual dimension; he is as funny as the day is long.

Justin has a benign contempt for me that actually manifests itself as a kind of affection. I'm just not a femme—his word for a certain kind of lady that he idolizes. (Femmes, you see, are a subgenre of women in general, all of whom he refers to as "smash-ups.") In any case, he is absolutely right—I am no femme: I don't sleep all day, as Aubrey does, and then emerge after sundown like a vampire; I never paint my nails; I don't own a garter belt or wear spike heels before nine P.M.; my hair is Joan of Arc short; I don't consider the cadging of drinks one of the lively arts; I don't share his and Aubrey's worship of Luther Vandross; and, probably my worst sin, I cannot shake my boody. The truth is, he thinks I'm overeducated and a secret dyke. Justin does not understand going to college and does *not* approve of lesbians. But he likes me in spite of himself and, giving the devil his due, he says my breasts are "amazing." We've been out drinking together a couple of times, once just the two of us and once with an old lover of mine, an Irishman who is still turning heads at age forty-two. Yeah, Tom Farrell garnered me quite a few Brownie points with Justin. On the other hand, Griffin, my ex, met Justin once, and the two of them scared each other half to death.

I saluted Justin, raising a phantom glass to his health, and continued walking backstage.

Aubrey gave out with one of those Patti LaBelle–register shrieks when she saw me swing through the door.

She was busy applying some kind of sparkly shit all over that flawless body and she didn't have a stitch on.

"Christ, Aubrey. Put some clothes on," I said. She made me feel like I had the body of a Sumo wrestler and the skin of Godzilla.

"This just makes my night! What are you doing here, sweetheart?" She slipped into a peach-colored robe as she spoke.

"I just thought I'd drop in for a minute on my way out to see Moms. Is there anything to drink back here?"

"Yeah, just a minute." She walked to the door and called out into the ether: "Larry, get me a Jack Daniels, baby. Tell him don't put no ice in it."

The glass was in my hand almost before I could blink. I took a healthy drink from it.

"You look kind of funny, Nan," she said. "Wait a minute . . . don't tell me that nigger is trifling with you again?"

"No, it's not Griff. It's my mother."

"How is Moms?" she asked me, back at her dressing table.

It was taking me a long time to answer. "What's the matter with her, Nan?"

"Probably nothing," I finally said.

"What does that mean?"

"I know you're going to say I'm crazy, but . . ." I repeated, a bit abashed, the phone message that had set me spinning.

"Nanette, you *are* crazy, girl. How you know it ain't something good instead of something terrible? She could be getting married again for all you know."

"Aubrey, I know you're a relentless optimist. But give me a break, huh. Moms is getting married? To who?"

"How do I know that?"

"Or me, for that matter."

"That's what I'm saying, Nan. You don't know all her business."

I took another deep drink of the bourbon. "Trust me, it's not wedding news."

"Okay, fool. She's not getting married. But that still don't mean she got cancer, do it?"

"No, you're right, it doesn't. But I'm still a little freaked. Which brings me to the reason—another reason—I came here. I thought if you could get a couple of hours off tonight, maybe you'd go out there with me."

"Oh shit. I can't, baby. I *am* taking some time off tonight—but I gotta meet somebody for a couple of hours."

"Oh." It flitted through my mind to ask who she was meeting, but then I remembered myself, and who I was talking to, and who she worked for. I didn't want to know any of the particulars. Of course, it might have been something perfectly innocent, but I thought I'd better let it go.

I stayed a few minutes longer, until it was almost time for her to go on again. She insisted on having one of the guys run me out to Queens in his car. I ran through my head the possibility of staring at the thick neck of some club gofer while I sat in the backseat all the way across town and then over the Long Island Expressway to Elmhurst. Or maybe, I thought with a shudder, he might try to chat me up. We'd talk about—what?—Heavy D's latest, or some new designer drug? My heart sank.

Then I mentally put myself on the subway, stop after stop after stop. I didn't even have a newspaper to distract me.

I went for the car.

I left with the promise that I would call her the next day to give her a full report on Mom's news, whatever it turned out to be.

On the way out I ran into Justin.

"What's happening, Smash-up?"

"Same old, same old, Justin. You know."

"Have a quick one with me, girlfriend."

"I can't."

"Got a date?"

"Yep. Dinner. With my mother."

"Ooooh. Bring me back some cornbread."

I guffawed. He didn't know how funny that was.

The kitchen was spotless, as always. But then, why shouldn't it be? Mom never cooked. Everything was take-out or pre-mixed or delivered in stay-warm aluminum foil.

"Mom, I'm here! Where are you?"

My mother's cotton dress was as surreal as the kitchen counters in its neatness. Decorous pageboy wig bobby-pinned in place. Makeup specially blended by one of the black salesladies at the Macy's in the mall.

It must be eight, nine years now since Daddy left her. But if I no longer remembered the exact date that had happened, Mom sure did. I bet she could tell you what she'd eaten for breakfast that day, what shoes Daddy was wearing when he broke the news to her. On those rare occasions when Mom talks about him, she never uses his name, referring to my father only as "him."

My father soon remarried: a young white teacher on his staff at the private school where he was now the principal. Outside of the occasional birthday lunch, Christmastime, and so on, I saw very little of him. He was happy enough, I suppose, in his new life. And he never missed an alimony payment.

"Nanette, what have you got on your feet?"

"They're called boots, Mother."

"Those things are something you wear down in the basement when you're looking to kill a rat. Don't tell me you dress like that for—"

"Holy mackerel, Mother, what is it you have to tell me!"

"It's about Vivian," she said grimly.

I fell into a chair, suddenly exhausted. No melanoma. Thank God. No wedding.

Vivian, my father's sister, had been my idol when I was a kid. Breezing into town and swooping me up, Aunt Vivian meant trips into Manhattan and eating exotic food and hanging with her hip friends and my first sip of beer and every other cool thing you can imagine when you're ten years old and your father's baby sister is a sophisticated sometime-fashion-model who drinks at piano bars and parties with people who actually make the rock 'n' roll records you hear on the radio.

My father felt about his little sister Vivian the way Justin feels about dykes. He disapproved of her friends and her nomadic ways and her prodigious consumption of vodka and her way-out hairdos and everything else about her lifestyle, which he didn't understand at all.

My mother didn't understand it any better than he did, but she loved Vivian just the same. Maybe that was due to the same kind of sympathy with strays that had moved her to take Aubrey to her heart. Mom looked on with pity while Auntie Viv blew all her money and drank too much and got her heart broken by trifling pretty men and then recovered to start the cycle all over again.

In time Vivian married and divorced—two or three times, if I remember right—and moved out of New York and then back again, half a dozen times—to L.A. and Mexico and France and Portugal—wherever the job or the party or the boyfriend might take her. Daddy and she finally had one final royal blowup during the cocaine-laced eighties and stopped speaking to each other altogether. We didn't even know where she had been living for the past eight or ten years.

And now, apparently, some disaster had befallen her.

"Is she dead?" I asked. "How did it happen?"

"No, no. She isn't dead."

"She isn't? Then what happened to her? What about Vivian?"

"She's in trouble. Wait here a minute."

Mom vanished into the dining room.

I sat looking around the kitchen in puzzlement, at last fixing on the covered Styrofoam plates that held our dinner, waiting to be popped into the microwave. And I thought the day had been long and weird *before* I crossed the bridge into Queens. What the hell was going on here? Well, at least my mother hadn't tried to reach me at NYU. That sure would have resulted in an interesting phone message. But I had always discouraged her from calling me at work, telling her that as a part-timer I didn't really have an office of my own.

"Look at these."

She handed me two pieces, one a standard tourist postcard with a corny photo of the Eiffel Tower, the other a telegram.

I turned the postcard over and read:

"Long time No see. Hate to ask you but I'm strapped. Can you spare anything? Just send what you can—if you can. Love, Viv."

The postmark on the card was about three weeks old.

There was an address beneath her signature. A place on the rue du Cardinal Lemoine—my Lord, Viv was in Paris.

I looked up at Mom and began to ask a question, but she ordered me to read the telegram first, which was dated a week or so after the postcard.

JEAN
DID YOU GET MY CARD?
WORSE. I CAN'T GET OUT.
VIV.

"What's this about?" I asked, the fear rising in my voice.

"I don't know, honey. I don't know." Her spine stiffened then and her eyes took on a glassy look. "I finally called . . . *him*. I mean, he is her brother."

"You're kidding! You called Daddy?"

She nodded.

I tried to imagine White Mrs. Daddy picking up the phone in their apartment near Lincoln Center. Handing the receiver over. Jesus, the look on his face when she told him who it was.

"What did he say?" I asked. "Did Viv write to him too?"

"Yes. But he doesn't want to know anything about Vivian. Says he tore the card up without reading it. It's a sin. I told him I hoped one day he would be hurting in the same way and when he reached out for help—well, never mind. I told him I think it's a sin, that's all."

I shook my head. "Wow. This is so weird. What are you going to do? You don't have any money to send her, and if Pop won't do it—"

"He wouldn't give it to her, but I managed to shame him into giving me something for you."

"*Me?* What do you mean?"

She pulled out a chair for herself then and sat down in it before answering. "Listen, Nan."

"What?"

"*I* don't have any money to spare. But—well, I do have it, but it's not mine. As a matter of fact it's Vivian's money."

"What are you talking about, Mother?"

"I mean I actually do have some money for Vivian—especially for her. When your grandfather died he left most of what he had to your daddy, naturally. And you got enough to take that beautiful trip. But you know how he was. He feuded with Viv just like your father did, but at the end he wanted to come to some kind of peace with her. Nobody even knew where Vivian was at the time. So he left her some money, and gave it to me to keep for her. It's in a special account. Waiting. There must be close to ten thousand in it by now."

"Ten thousand dollars! That sure sounds like enough to

bail her out of trouble. And you mean you've had this money all along?"

"Yes. I knew sooner or later we'd hear from her again."

"But not like this," I said.

"No. Not like this. And so . . ." She glanced away from me then.

"What is it?"

"I know it's a lot to ask, Nan. You haven't seen Viv since you were a kid. I just know she's over there drinking, broke, stranded somewhere. Maybe even sick. I wouldn't know where to begin to help her. I don't know how I'd even get out of the airport over there. But I thought—since you've been there so many times—I thought maybe you could go over there and help her— take this money to her and help her get home. Like I said, I managed to shame your father into giving me enough for your expenses."

Expenses?

"What are you saying, Mother? You want me to go to Paris!"

"Yes. Would you do it? If—I mean, only if you could take the time from work. You're going to be on spring vacation soon, aren't you?"

"It started yesterday, Mom. No problem."

A lot to ask! *Holy*—

I felt a kick right then. Right on the shin. I knew who that was: my conscience, Ernestine. I just kicked the bitch right back. Yes, I'm a liar, I told her; a deceiver, a cold-hearted Air France slut. I was thinking not of my Aunt Viv in a French drunk tank but of the braised rabbit in that bistro on the rue Monsieur le Prince.

A lot to ask? Coq au vin, here I come!

CHAPTER 2

Can't We Be Friends?

I know I'm a fool. A sentimentalist. A sucker for a sad song. The same old hokey things undo me every time.

I was crying so hard I could barely see out the window of the taxi, one of those workhorse Renaults with a driver who smoked Gitanes, a beautifully dappled Dalmatian asleep beside him on the front seat. It was April and the trees were budding and we had just passed the Arc de Triomphe and it was tearing my heart out.

It helped a lot that I had sucked down about fifty glasses of Veuve Clicquot on the flight over and been hit on big time by both an African diplomat in a vintage Armani and a sublimely big-nosed Frenchman.

Drying my eyes, I recalled that first time I saw Paris, from the window of a train. I was still a student and traveling on the cheap. I took a charter flight into Amsterdam, where I met up with a couple of classmates and their European boyfriends. After a couple of days of museum going and smoking pot till I was pixillated, I took the train into Paris. That first sight of the roof of the Gare de Nord, alive with pigeons, had produced the same kind of waterworks.

By the time the cab deposited me at the picturesque little square in the 5th arrondissement, I was working on one hell of a hangover. The address on Vivian's postcard turned out to be a clean but decidedly unglamorous little hotel at the top of a rise in the pavement. Their one-star rating was not mere modesty—nothing fancy about the place. I set my valise down and walked over to the *reception*.

There was no such American madame as Vivian Hayes registered at the hotel, the well-fed gentleman behind the desk reported. Perhaps my friend was at the small hotel at the other end of the square? No, I said, checking the postcard again, this was the address given. It occurred to me then that Aunt Viv might be using either of two—or was it three?—married names. So I began to describe her, thinking even as I did so that she had probably changed so much since our last meeting that the description might be worthless. I was just about to dig into my bag for a twenty-year-old snapshot of Vivian, when the monsieur suddenly realized who I was seeking.

A sneer pulled at his lips. "Oh yes. I recall your friend now." I waited for him to go on. "This Madame Hayes," he said contemptuously, had checked out more than ten days ago.

"Checked out" was not exactly the phrase he used to describe her departure. Apparently Vivian had left without paying the last week's rent, abandoning her suitcase and clothing and personal items. She had simply gone out one afternoon and never returned.

Not good.

I had counted on some kind of trouble. Still, I didn't have to hit the panic button yet. I might have to mount a search for her. On the other hand, she might be able to raise a few dollars from somewhere, in which case she would show up again to pay her bill and collect her things.

But I couldn't think about that at the moment. My head was pounding and I needed some sleep—real sleep, not airplane nodding. This hotel was not exactly what I'd had in mind as a base of operations, but it would do for now. Hell, dowdy French hotels short on amenities but rich in character had been the sites of some of my most delightful adventures.

I asked for a room and, to forestall any problems, paid for a few days in advance. I pulled the envelope with the Thomas Cook money orders earmarked for Aunt Vivian out of my carry-on bag and committed it to the hotel safe. Mom had asked if it wouldn't be better to buy traveler's checks in my own name, but I wanted to guarantee I wouldn't be tempted to start dipping into those funds for my own use. In Vivian's place, I don't think I would've appreciated any messenger messing about with my inheritance, even if it was a totally unexpected gift from heaven.

I splurged on the best room in the house. Even so, the toilet was down the hall. The bidet had been cracked and repaired half a dozen times. The bureau smelled faintly of mildew. But the room was a good size, and the view wasn't bad. Not bad at all: my room, on the sixth floor, looked out over the busy square with its ancient copper fountain. I put in five minutes at the open window just looking at the people, pulling the air into my chest—and thinking about Aunt Vivian, somewhere out there. I didn't know yet what kind of shape I'd find her in. But I did know she wouldn't be high stepping in her designer jeans and smart black pumps. She wouldn't be laughing her tantalizing laugh that put lights in her clear brown eyes. She wouldn't be young anymore.

I thought, too, of my first trip to Paris and all the subsequent ones; of the friends I'd once had here, all dispersed to other places, other lives, now; of my summer in Provence; the meals, the men; the just plain fun. I'd been happy, ecstatic, in Paris—drunk on it—and yet I'd also known that peculiar *tristesse* that could fasten around your heart like a vise, for no particular reason, and suddenly make you feel so very alone.

Tiredness overtook me then. I closed the shutters tight. I turned back the covers on the creaky iron bed and slipped between the ironed white sheets. And then—darkness.

The trick is not to let yourself sleep too long lest you fall victim to jet lag. It was the only travel tip I could ever remember. You've got to crash and allow the old ankles to lose the swelling that results from sitting constricted in one place for so long. Nap, yes. But you mustn't sleep too long, or you'll be on the way back home before your body clock is running right again.

I was groggy when I pulled myself out of dreamland—and ravenous. I opened the metal shutters. *Pam!* Night had fallen. Those inimitable lights were all around me, and, down below, the canopies of a thousand cafes. I went and cleaned up quickly in the communal shower room and then jumped into some black trousers and a leotard. I threw my long raincoat over that and I was ready to roll.

I did a quick turn around the Pantheon, where I had often gone in the dark of night to sit and think and sometimes consume a couple of *boules* of rich ice cream purchased at one of the carts dotting the landscape. Then I headed back across the square and the boulevard St. Michel, pulsating with young people.

I hit boulevard St. Germain, or rather it hit me. It was Friday night and the street was hopping. Traffic was the predictable nightmare. I took a deep breath and ran, snaked, bullied my way across the street, heedless of the color of the traffic lights. I headed north then, away from the worst of the crowds. I had decided to eat at the Café Cloche, which was on the pricey side, but my mouth was watering for a couple of their beautiful spring lamb chops. I remembered that they didn't take reservations— the only reason I had for believing I'd get a table on a Friday night. The cross streets were beginning to look familiar now. Yes, this was the block. The café was near.

Except it wasn't. It was not there. The Café Cloche, where I'd once been seduced by a chain-smoking academic from Toulouse over a fine *daube* of beef, was no more. I stared stupidly, dejected, at the darkened window of the boutique that had replaced the restaurant.

Well, what was the big deal? Things change. So I'd find someplace else to eat dinner. A restaurant closing was a small thing, yet, inexplicably, it unsettled me. I walked back slowly into the heart of the crowd and found a friendly looking if undistinguished place where I ordered foie gras and then went on to langoustines and a half bottle of white wine. Afterward, I browsed somnolently through a few of the late-night bookstores on St. Michel, buying nothing, and found my way back to the hotel.

I got into my nightgown almost immediately. It was cool in the room but I opened the window wide and let the low night sky fall in on me. Another one of those singular Paris moments. The lights on the Pantheon were silver blue and I watched them for a long time, wondering how many others were doing the same thing, their hearts moving in their chest. But, curiously enough, I had stopped crying.

I made a bet with myself as I called downstairs to order breakfast. At every hotel I'd ever lived in on this side of the Seine, the maid's name was Josette. I figured that would never change.

I lost. Marise bid me good morning in her musical colonial accent—was she from Antigua? maybe St. Croix?—and set the wooden tray bearing my soupy black coffee and croissants down at the foot of the bed.

I spent the late morning and all afternoon checking out the really low-rent hotels on streets like Gay Lussac, thinking that Vivian might have got her hands on a few bucks to live on, but not enough to go back to the hotel in the Square. The next day, I figured, I'd go another rung down on the ladder and try Pigalle and the parts of Bastille that had not yet been gentrified. Then, if I didn't turn up any leads, I'd head out to the edge of the city,

Buttes Chaumont or someplace, where I'd probably be mugged and left for dead somewhere.

I put in a full day. Nothing. At six o'clock I returned to the hotel and put in a call to my mother, reporting on my progress, or rather lack of progress.

I took a long soak in the pay-per-bath room down the hall and changed into something slightly slinky. There was a fabulous wine bar on the rue du Cherche Midi that I loved. It had been the scene of two or three major flirting triumphs.

They sold lighting fixtures there now. I stood on the pavement watching the clerk clear the register and begin to close up for the evening. I could have cried.

I wandered down into the métro and took the train to Pont Marie, on the right bank. Surely the much more staid wine bar that a friend's father had once taken us to would still be there. And it was. But it was obvious there would be no lighthearted seductions taking place that evening. Oh no. No sharing a steak frites with a cute translator and then a nightcap at some avant garde jazz loft. No and no. Average age of the patrons at this stately establishment: 55 by my calculations. Successful businessmen and their co-workers, or their Chanel-clad ladies. I put away two lovely glasses of Medoc and was on my way.

I walked along the Seine in the twilight, feet hurting in my strappy heels. The magazine/postcards/junk stands on the quai were all closed now. Here and there I could hear voices down below, along the water. I had to smile. One thing you never forget, your first kiss on the banks of the Seine. I just know it's one of those pictures that go flying across your vision as you lay dying.

I had had nothing to eat except the breakfast croissant and a yogurt taken on the run midday. I was starving but I hated the thought of eating alone again.

What choice did I have, though? I went to Au Pactole, a perfectly nice place on St. Germain, just the tiniest bit stuffy, up the block from a hotel I'd once lived in—the Hotel de Lima. It was almost pleasurable to behave so formally with the maître d', like playing a role, or wearing a disguise. *Hmmm—she is black and French speaking. Must be an immigrant. Spinster on vacation from the provinces,* I could almost hear the young waiter thinking. *Trying to dress Parisian. Not bad looking. Needs to get laid, though.* I was the only solo table in the good-sized room, which was awash in fresh white flowers and skyscraper-tall candles. After an already too heavy meal, I pigged on goat cheese and a big-time dessert.

The thing is, I mused during my meandering walk home along the quai, the main thing is: the police have to be avoided.

If nothing happened with my search for Vivian in the next day or so, I might have to contact the American embassy. But not the French police. It was half instinctual cop-o-phobia and half worry that maybe Vivian had wandered into something not on the up and up; then there was the plain gut-clenching terror based on the Gallic mind-set. Guilty until proven innocent was not a metaphor over here, it was the law. You just did not fuck with cops in this country—not even traffic cops.

What does a foreigner do when he or she is broke, in trouble—no friends, no resources? I didn't know. True, I had bummed around Europe before, hitchhiked with companions, smoked dope with kids I met at discos, and so on. But I had never been anything like stranded or in trouble with the law. I always had a return ticket in my pocket, and help was a collect call away. I thought about the asshole white boys who thought they were slick enough to get away with smuggling hashish out of Turkey. I found myself shuddering.

The *Herald Tribune?* What about placing an ad there—"Aunt Viv: You're richer than you think. Call home. All is forgiven." Something to that effect.

Not a likely venue. Vivian had lived in Paris before. She had enough French that if she read the newspapers at all, she'd read a French one.

I was at the Pont Neuf. Shit, I had been so lost in my thoughts that I'd overshot the hotel. I was beat, my toes crying out for release.

Give me your tired, your poor . . . your Manolo Blahniks . . . your tart tatin.

Not just tired now. I was slappy. Maybe I hadn't escaped the jet lag after all. I stood on the quai for a few minutes more. Well, good night, old Notre Dame. And if it's not too much trouble, help me find Aunt Viv before I have to go to the 19th. Amen.

I visited at least fifteen fleabag hotels and hostels the next day. I was seeing the side of Paris they don't print up on the picture postcards. The homeless, the druggies, the bag ladies, the nut jobs were nowhere near as numerous, as filthy, or as desperate as their New York cousins, but they did nothing for tourism either.

Just to make myself feel less like a mendicant, I went and had lunch in an overpriced, overdecorated restaurant in Montmartre and then took the funicular up to Sacré Coeur. I looked out over the city while the shutterbugs swarmed all around me. Maybe there is a heaven, I thought, and it's nothing more than these rooftops.

As long as I was doing the American in Paris bit, I figured I'd go to American Express, on the very remote chance that Vivian had left a message there. Of course, she'd have to know I was in Paris. But what did I have to lose? Perhaps she had spoken to my mother by now.

No such luck. And now I was stuck in the busy 9th, clogged with crazed shoppers and sightseers, the traffic like a million killer bees. I had to admit, the Opéra was looking a great deal spiffier than the last time I'd been in Paris. Choking on exhaust and too weary to do any window shopping of my own, I zigzagged across the boulevard des Capucines and went down into the métro station.

Home at last, thank the baby Jesus. The alert, generous-bosomed madame who seemed to rule at the hotel was having her afternoon *tisane* when I stopped at the desk for my key. I must have looked about as frazzled as I felt, because she offered me a cup.

French businesswomen are about the least homey human beings imaginable. Anybody would be scared of them. I know I am. This one, however, told me she had noticed my saxophone, and wondered if I was in Paris to play an engagement somewhere. She had always admired *le jazz*, she said, and at the time of their wedding anniversary each year, she and her husband enjoyed making an evening of it at the music club just off St. Germain des Pré. You know—the one with the likeness of Satchmo in black plaster in the entryway.

I told the madame, in as little detail as possible, about my search for Aunt Viv. She was sympathetic—genuinely so, I believed—and when she offered further assistance, I jumped on it.

The madame's husband relieved her at the desk while the two of us climbed into the taxi she had ordered. We were going to La Pitié Salpêtrière, a giant medical complex in the 13th arrondissement that also housed the city morgue. It made sense, didn't it, to check there first? Oh yes, it was quite sensible, my companion agreed. After all, if, heaven forbid, Vivian was at La Pitié, then there was little point in canvassing the hospitals and the emergency rooms and hospices and so on—our search would be over.

The office where we waited had a beautiful view of the Jardin des Plantes. As the lady from the administrative office led us along the corridors the worst kinds of morbid one-liners were running through my brain. I couldn't help it. It was like whistling in the graveyard.

Back in the fresh air, I went weak with relief, happy to know that Viv was not one of the bodies in those human filing cabinets. The madame and I rested for a few moments on a bench in the Jardin des Plantes and then caught another cab home.

Back at the hotel we worked out a fair way of computing the phone charges I was racking up calling the appropriate municipal offices to determine if anyone fitting my aunt's general description had been admitted to a Paris hospital. It seemed only right, I told her gratefully, that I also pay the week's rent that my aunt had skipped on. That was most responsible of me, she said. Would I like to pay that now, or should she add that sum to my own bill at the end of my stay?

None of the hospitals had any mysterious amnesiacs in residence who might be my poor aunt. So, as far as we knew, Aunt Vivian was still alive, somewhere out there. She had to be. If she was broke, how was she going to get out of Paris? I was going to have to bite the bullet and go to the embassy soon, it seemed.

It was time for me to clear out of Madame's way and let her get her dinner started. I thanked her for all her efforts—the tea and sympathy not the least of them—and went upstairs.

About seven o'clock I put on a fresh shirt and jeans and left the hotel, with no particular destination.

I wound up at one of the revival cinemas near the place everybody referred to as the Beat Hotel, a dump with character over on the rue Gît le Coeur, which I had checked out the previous day. Its reputation had been made by William Burroughs and his crowd in the fifties, and I guess its legend was still going strong. Not a single vacancy.

The street was clogged with kids of all nations, hanging out, playing guitars, smoking reefer, dry humping in doorways, eating *frites* and souvlaki, and just glorying in being alive and young and stupid. A few paces away was perhaps the world's narrowest, shortest street, which I had searched for years ago, on my first visit to the city, because its name was so intriguing: rue de Chat-Qui-Peche. The Cat Who Fishes? What the hell was the point of that? Right after finding it, I had had an even bigger disappointment. I had wandered over to the rue Mouffetard, where, I had been told, a lot of cute third world students ate cheap Middle Eastern meals. I was promptly groped and nearly kidnapped by a tobacconist with hideous b.o., and had never again set foot on that street.

At least the movie was no disappointment. How many times had I seen *Children of Paradise* since my college roommate and I first caught it on campus? Too many to count. I cried again anyway.

Lord, what a beautiful night. There was no way I was going to dinner alone again. Maybe I should turn into the first bar I saw and make a fool of myself by begging some stranger to come eat with me—or perhaps I should just pick up a sandwich someplace and call it a night.

I went for the sandwich. I would not have been good company for anybody.

After coffee the next morning an idea came to me. No, I hadn't yet thought of my next move for locating Vivian. It was something a lot goofier than that.

In fact, it was probably about the goofiest idea that had ever come my way: I decided to take my sax down into the métro and play for change. Reckless. Silly. Ill-considered. Preposterous.

Formidable, I'd do it.

It was the stuff of fantasy. Maybe I didn't have the chops a lot of my fellow street musicians back in Manhattan had, but at least I'd be able to say I played in Paris. I got cleaned up and dressed in a hurry. I wanted to get out of the room and down into the métro before I had a chance to wimp out.

I got a polite *bonjour* along with an indulgent smile from the old monsieur behind the reception desk as I tripped past him, my instrument case festooned with an old India print scarf I often use as a strap for the sax.

I bought a booklet of métro tickets and passed through the turnstile. It was an act of supreme hubris to set up shop at Odéon, one of the busier stops in the city. What with the number of hip Parisians who lived in or passed through the neighborhood every day——students, intellectuals, musicians, jazzaholics of all stripes——I was betting half of them had heard better horns than mine before they'd finished their morning coffee.

But what the hell. I wasn't playing to pay the rent; I was living out a fantasy. I settled myself at the mouth of the passageway connecting the Clignancourt line to the Austerlitz, took a deep breath, and started to blow. I began with "How Deep Is the Ocean." Hardly anyone took notice of me. That was okay, because my playing was a lot rustier than my French. I didn't sound so great.

Still, I pressed on. I chose "With a Song in My Heart" next. Not bad, if I do say so myself. And indeed, a cool-looking man in an expensive trench coat stood there attentively until I'd finished, and then began to dig into his pocket for change. The sound of the francs hitting the bottom of the case made my heart soar. I gave the guy a big shit-eating grin and immediately launched into "Lover Man." I felt so good, anything seemed possible. Maybe even a certifiable miracle. Maybe I'd see Viv bustling along the tunnel, running to catch a train.

The late morning crowd was replaced by the noontime one, people bustling along to lunch appointments, or going to do their shopping, or heading home for a leisurely meal and maybe some quick nooky——or vice versa——before returning to work.

I had to chuckle at the idea I'd had earlier in the morning—that if I kept at it all day, maybe I could make enough in tips to buy Moms and Aubrey some nice perfume. Ha. I barely made enough to buy a Big Mac. It really didn't bother me, though. I was having a good time.

I went above ground about two o'clock and found a cart that had nice-looking crêpes. I strolled along the Seine as I ate, and then turned into a beautiful old tabac on the Quai Voltaire, where I had a *grand café* and bummed a cigarette from a waiter who was tall enough for the NBA and weighed about ten pounds.

I couldn't wait to get back to my post in the subway. And when I did, I hit the ground running. I had never managed to make "It Never Entered My Mind" sound like that before in my life. And my "Green Dolphin Street" ran a close second. I even got a nice round of applause from a group of older women with folding umbrellas.

Don't *ever* get too comfortable. It's just one of a thousand lessons that I have never truly taken in. My mother has been cautioning me about it since I was old enough to crawl. And Ernestine, my conscience, never tires of saying it. But I always forget.

It was about five-thirty. I got through a couple of bars of "You Took Advantage of Me" before I realized something strange was up. I was hearing the same licks being played—note for note—not twenty feet away. On a violin, of all things. It startled the shit out of me. In fact, for a moment I thought I was hallucinating. I looked into the passageway and saw a long-legged, light-skinned black man with demure dreadlocks and wire-rim spectacles gazing directly, defiantly into my eyes while he bowed absentmindedly.

I stood where I was, seething, until he finished, and then strode over to the gangly Caribbean-looking prick. "What the fuck do you think you're doing? I was here first," I told him in rapid-fire French.

His eyes bugged behind the glass of his spectacles.

"*Idiot!*" I shouted at him. And then went on to ask him if he was deaf, and then if he was under the mistaken impression that he was funny. I finished with "Who the hell do you think you are—Marcel Marceau?"

There was plenty of anger in his eyes, but he said nothing. Which only increased my fury.

"*Eh bien, salaud? Pourquoi tu me reponds pas?*"

"I'm not answering you," he said, acidly, and in English, "because I don't know any gutter French yet."

"Oh my God. You're . . . an American."

At this point he chose to answer me in French, adding a Gallic smirk to his little repertory of expressions: "No need to be so snotty about it. So are you—obviously."

"Obviously?" I began to splutter. "Oh, so *I* don't know how to speak French? Is that what your lame-ass little riposte is supposed to mean?"

More smirk.

I got right up in his face then. "Don't even think about criticizing my accent, mister. You speak French like a pig."

"That's because I am an autodidact. I hope to polish my accent while—"

"An *au-to-di-dact*," I repeated, and then began to roar with scornful laughter. I was being the schoolyard bully picking on the kid with the bulging book bag. It was cheap and unworthy of me, but I couldn't put the brakes on it. "Jesus, this is unbelievable. I have to come all the way to Paris to deal with an evil, pretentious, bourgeois asshole from the hood—"

"I was thinking the same thing about you."

"Hey, you see here! I may be pretentious, but I am *not* bourgeois—and I sure as hell am not from *your* hood."

"Bitch, you can be from Jupiter for all I care," he said, abruptly ending our absurd argument. "Just as long as you move your ass along. This is my spot."

"What do you mean, your spot? You own it or something?"

"I mean I got a right to play here at this time four days a week. I have a piece of paper that says so."

"I don't believe you."

"I have no interest in what you believe. I'm a legal resident of the city of Paris and I have an artist permit to play here."

I was going to slice into him about his prissy-sissy attitude, but suddenly all the wind was gone from my sails. Suddenly I knew who I reminded myself of: a monster-gold-earring-wearing gangsta girl on the IRT; hunching her shoulders, threatening, gesticulating wildly, using her high-polished fingernails like a garden trowel as she read out some enemy in subliterate slang.

"You know what?" I said, calm now. "You can die on this fucking spot, mister legal resident. Forget you."

I turned on my heel and walked back to my case.

As I climbed the stair at the other end of the tunnel, I could hear him playing "How About You?"

His playing was effortless, swinging, like something humming inside your own head.

I'd like to show you some New York in June, I thought bitterly.

Oh, but shit, he was good.

Well, that was nice and ugly.

"Ugly" didn't really capture the essence of it, though. It was, to use some prissy language of my own, mortifying. Jesus—why did I do that!

I hated myself.

Above ground again, my face burned with shame. Two black Americans, strangers, meeting in Paris under those singularly strange circumstances—it should have been an occasion for rejoicing. But what do we do? Rather, what do I do? Ridicule. Curse. Clown. Fight over a little patch of pee-soaked concrete. Goddamn, it was horrible. And the more I thought about it, the more thoroughly depressed I became.

I walked for a while, trying to get myself in hand, shake off the bad feelings. I sat in the Jardins du Luxembourg for a little while, smelling the sweetness of the grass, despising it. I watched the parents as they sauntered home with their kids; the lovers as they kissed in parting. Everybody seemed to be carrying a baguette for that night's dinner. Man, it would be so nice to be invited to somebody's house for dinner. I was yearning for somebody just to call me by my name—for something familiar like that. A plain meal in an apartment I'd visited many times, and a couple of hours of aimless, civilized conversation. I am still civilized, I told myself. Despite that appalling interlude in the métro. I'm not the asshole who behaved that way. I'm better than that—really.

I went and had a drink at the Café Flore. In fact, I had a few of them.

Like every musician, probably, I had often wondered what it was like to play high on drugs. All the cornball stuff crosses your mind: does the heroin unlock some door in your soul? Does it make you better? I don't just mean, does it make you play better. I mean, are *you* better, however briefly.

For all my musical forefathers, it had to do more than just make the pain go away. God. Negroes and their pain. What the fuck were we going to do if suddenly it all did go away? Would we even know who we were anymore?

The waiter was looking at me, the bottle in his left hand, the smile on his lips like a question mark.

I shook my head. No more, *merci*.

I wasn't exactly merry, but I'd had enough wine to make me lighten up somewhat. Enough with the clichés, Nan, I cautioned myself. No more being blue in Paris. Gotta lose that "Azure-tay," as Nat Cole sang.

So, back to work. I walked for a few blocks and then descended into the station called St. Sulpice. The crowds had disappeared. I set up and began to play again. Not many passersby, but what did it matter? The sounds of my horn ricocheted hauntingly off the tiled walls. I felt almost as though I was in my own private city, the occasional visitor dropping a few francs into my case like a toll to enter the gates.

I played "Something to Live For" and another Ellington, "Come Sunday."

I think what happened was, I pushed it too far. One minute I was playing the break on "Ill Wind," my eyes closed, and the next moment I was seeing stars. I had thought I heard a kind of scuffling noise farther down the tunnel, but I was so wrapped up in playing I paid no attention.

All I know is that suddenly they were on me: two white guys in denim and swastika-ed leather, short haircuts, bad teeth. And one of them was banging my head against the tiles.

I began to flail around, hit out blindly, but my fists never connected with anything. I became dimly aware of shouting—somewhere far off—and then I heard a ripping sound. They were tearing the pockets off my jeans, going after my money, I guess. The instrument case must have gotten overturned, because the few coins that had been inside it, I heard rolling up the tunnel floor. Someone was pulling at the strap of the sax now, but it was all twisted around my head. I heard the unmistakable epithet, *negre*, spoken through clenched teeth as I took a blow to the face. I once saw a film clip of Thelonious Monk playing at the Five Spot in New York. When the spirit moved him, he got up from the piano and spun himself around madly, like a holy drunk. That's how I felt right then, as if someone had set me spinning, like Monk, and I was never going to stop.

My head and heart were drumming hard. I raised my hands to cover my ears. Something on my face. Something on my hands. Wet. That was blood. Blood! Was I cut up?

So this is how it ends, I thought fleetingly. Me beaten to death by skinheads. Aunt Viv starves to death in a back alley or rots in prison. Mother, grief stricken, carted off screaming to the insane asylum. Daddy, riddled with guilt, commits suicide. Negro angst turned Wagnerian.

"Ends" is the right word. One of them is coming back to finish me off now. His face comes into focus. Wish I had the strength to kick him in the balls.

But wait—it's not a white face. And this guy's got a mop of curly hair and wears glasses.

And, somehow, all the noise has stopped.

CHAPTER 3

I Didn't Know About You

White sheets. Creaky bedsprings. My old suitcase open on top of the bureau. Unless heaven was a budget hotel room with no TV, I was still alive.

Oh yes. There was something else in my room that tipped me off I wasn't dead: a fine-looking, long-legged, high yellow black man, snoring softly, sitting on a hard chair, his big bare feet propped up at the foot of my bed. He wasn't wearing any pants. Gray T-shirt over matching briefs.

Lord-a-muzzy, I am still alive.

"How's it going, sleeping beauty?"

Shit. He caught me staring at his shorts. How gross.

"I'm okay, I think. My nose hurts a little. Is it broken?"

"Nothing broken," he said, a little patronizing.

There followed a long and awkward silence.

"Last night's still fuzzy to you, I guess," he said, yawning and getting to his feet. He reached for his trousers and turned his back while he zipped up. "I asked if you wanted to go to the hospital, but you wouldn't do it."

"Yeah, one member of the family in trouble is enough," I mumbled.

"What?"

"Doesn't matter. I remember now. You rescued me and got me back here."

He didn't respond. Instead, he went over to the basin and began to splash water on his face.

"Damn nice of you," I said, laughing a bit, too embarrassed to do much else. "After that scene I pulled—going out on you like that in the métro—you should have let them kill me."

He shook his head. "Forget it."

"God, I haven't even asked, how are you? What are you—Hercules or something? There were two of those freaks. Did they hurt you?"

"Not really. I'm not much of a hero. I was screaming like a white lady and three or four other folks came running to help us out. The Aryan League didn't even manage to get your wallet."

I suddenly buried my face in my hands and moaned.

"What is it?" he said, alarmed. "Headache?"

"No, no, no. I'm just cursing my fucking karma. I don't know why I'm so surprised when stuff like this happens to me. You know what I mean?"

"Uh—"

"What's the story downstairs, by the way? Did you bring me in here all bloody and stuff? And what did they say—'Be out by tomorrow morning'?"

"I told them I witnessed two thugs trying to rob you.

The madame is the one who supplied the sleeping pill for you."

"Oh."

"Why did you ask that?" I distinctly heard lofty censure in his voice. "You think they figure anything that happens to a black person, it's gotta be his own fault? Some flour-faced Nazis just tried to kill you. Why are you worried about how it looks to some white people? Think you're letting the race down?"

Oooh. Touched a nerve there. Big time.

She's a little middle-class hypocrite playing the bohemian. Was that what he was thinking? What did we have here? A truly enlightened brother? Or was he mixing me up with himself? Was he talking about his own fears? Or had he really zeroed in on mine?

I decided discretion was the better part of etcetera and—for once—held my tongue.

"All right," I said. "You nailed me trying to be exemplary. I've been chastened, and you paid me back for what I said about you being bourgeois, okay? But it's a little more complicated than that. The management here is just not having the best luck with the coloreds from Elmhurst, Queens lately."

He looked at me questioningly but didn't press for any explanations.

The silence fell again. "How about handing me that mirror?" I finally asked.

He plucked my makeup mirror from the bureau top and gave it to me. He stood at the foot of the bed quietly examining me while I examined my face. He was right: nothing broken. The bridge of my nose was a bit tender and there was a little lump on the back of my head. That was all. I didn't look half as bad as I imagined. In fact, the tonic effect of a good night's sleep seemed to be right there on my face. Satisfied, I nodded and handed the mirror back.

"Think you're going to be okay now?" he asked.

"Fine."

"Good. I just didn't want to leave you until I was sure."

"Listen," I called out to him as he prepared to leave, "you *do* have a place to stay, right? I mean, you really are living—uh—somewhere?"

I saw that little smirk on his lips.

"Yes. I don't need any help."

"Right, right," I said quickly. "I kind of forgot for a minute there. I'm the one who needs all the help." *You're Mr. Perfect, aren't you, you prick?* Damn, was there nothing I could do right with this guy? He just kept outclassing me. He was a living reminder of my incompetence. Bet if he was looking for his aunt Vivian she'd be cleaned up and firmly in hand by now, her ass in a seat on TWA.

"What's your name?" he asked mildly.

I began to laugh then. That's right. We hadn't been introduced, had we?

"Nan."

"My name's Andre."

"Okay. Thanks again, Andre. I owe you one."

"You really do speak French very well," he said.

"I've got an idea, Andre. Why don't you start polishing your accent, like you said yesterday. Why don't you pick up the phone there and order two breakfast trays with extra coffee."

I got one thing right, at last. Cheerful little Marise, the maid, was sick that day. Her replacement was indeed called Josette. She had never served me before, so she didn't even raise an eyebrow at finding two of us in the room.

I carefully moved his violin case aside and opened the shutters wide to let in the morning air.

"Keep polishing, Andre. Speak to me in French," I said, pouring more coffee.

"I don't know if I can hold up my end all in French," he said.

"That's okay. Do the best you can." I then began to speak in my senior-year seminar French accent, enunciating clearly but keeping my vocabulary colloquial, everyday: "First off, tell me what you're doing over here, if it's any of my business. Are you in school?"

"No. I got a little bit of money after my mother died—insurance—and I just headed straight over here. I'm planning to be . . ."

"Be what?" I asked when he hesitated.

"Famous maybe."

I cracked up.

"Well, you sure can play that violin. Is that what's going to make you famous?"

"Yeah. Well, yes and no. I want to do something with the music, sure. But I'm also taking notes for this book I'm thinking about writing."

"No kidding? What kind of book?"

"About black people in Paris. Musicians mostly, but others too—dancers, soldiers, poets, whoever I come across. And not just the big ones like Josephine Baker and Wright and them. I mean people who worked to get over here and would do anything to stay. They were excited—proud to be here. Not like tourists, you know? Like there was something really at stake for them. People like me." He paused there. "And you."

I couldn't help it. I was fucking happy he had included me.

"I want to walk around in their footsteps," he continued, "look up their friends and families, if they had any, visit the places where they lived. Give them their due. It's hard to do something like that—start over in a strange place. Hard. Lonely. Scary. There's more than one way to be a black hero—to me, anyway. I want to tell people how admirable some of those folks were."

"*Formidable*," I said. "So there is a little of the race man in you after all."

His face went scarlet around the edges. But, thankfully, he laughed rather than bristled.

"Where'd you study music?" I asked.

"I went to Curtis."

"You're from Philadelphia?"

"No. Detroit, originally." There was a sourish expression on his face.

"Sounds like you didn't like it much."

He shrugged. "Wasn't just Detroit. I didn't like anything that much in the States."

"I can hear that," I said.

I wanted to say something more than that, but I couldn't quite form the words yet. The permutations of our relationship to the whole of America were endless. You could hate white people but not hate America. You could come to terms with the racism but never accept the insipid culture. You could view our disenfranchisement as a kind of massive swindle—all that blood, sorrow, loyalty, hope, and patience deposited over the centuries, and the check keeps bouncing. You could simply self-destruct. Like I said, endless. I figured I'd hear the particulars of his take on the thing soon enough.

"Like Baldwin said, 'I had to get out before I killed somebody.' Is that how you felt?"

"Something like that," he answered, not looking at me. "More than likely, if anybody was gonna end up dead, it would have been me. Like I told you before, I'm hardly anybody's idea of fierce. Keep in mind that when I was little I used to have to walk home carrying a violin. *And* these thick glasses. It was like wearing a sign that said KICK THE SHIT OUT OF ME."

"Kids are real nice to each other, aren't they?" I said, chuckling, but angry too. I was thinking about my friend Aubrey's treatment at the hands of some of our peers. "Who was it that saw your musical stuff and put you in school?"

"My mother. She could talk you out of your teeth. Got me scholarships to everything. We didn't have much. My father died when I was seven."

"What was she like, your mother?"

"White. Which made things even more interesting than they might have been."

Yeah, I thought as much. Aggressive as our DNA is, there were still little hints of the other in his face. "Tell me more," I said.

I divided the last of the coffee between our two cups. Boy! did I want a cigarette.

"Well, like they say, nothing lasts forever," he said. "You get over yourself, one way or another. I stopped running from fights. And the fellas stopped wanting to fight me around the time we all discovered sex. See, the girls liked me."

I grinned. "Yaaay, Andre! So you went from being the four-eyed sissy to the neighborhood pussy magnet."

"You got it. For however brief a time, I was a hero."

"Fierce at last!" I raised the fist to him.

"No, I told you, I'm not. But I'll tell you who was. My mom. I don't know how she did it, exactly, but she's the one who—" He stopped there and didn't talk again until he had drained his cup.

When he spoke again, his voice had become thick. "A lot of things make me want to kill. And a lot of things I just don't give a fuck about anymore. All I care about now is becoming excellent at my work and being legit over here. Getting my papers, steady gigs, an apartment, whatever. 'Cause I am *not* going back. By the way, that was a load of crap I gave you about being a legal resident and having a permit, just in case you didn't already know.

"About the only thing that makes me want to fight now is other people telling me who I am and what I ought to be doing and who I ought to be doing it with."

"You mean you don't like having your blackness challenged?"

"My blackness is not open to challenge. My father was black, so that means I'm black. Period. I guess what I mean is, my people deserve to be honored by me, and I'm serious about doing that—but I deserve some honor too, right? Who doesn't?"

"Yeah," I said. "Who doesn't? Are you all on your own now? No family?"

"No."

"How long have you been in Paris?"

"Five months."

"Made any friends yet?"

He shook his head. "Not really. Just some guys I met playing around town. The place I'm staying at belongs to one of my profs, but he isn't there now. I'm subletting from him."

"What are you—"

He cut me off. "Just a minute! Hold up! Question after question after question. We're only talking about me. I want to know something about you and your stuff."

"You will, you will," I said. "Tell you what. Wait for me in the café downstairs while I get ready."

"Ready for what?"

"We're going to get seriously drunk."

"Are you joking?"

"Seriously, intentionally drunk."

"It's only ten-thirty," he said giddily. "In the morning."

"I know. But I'm about to tell you my life story, right? That's not something you do sober, my brother. And you've got to show me your Paris before I show you mine."

He picked up his violin and practically danced over to the door.

"It's good to be an international nigger, don't you find, Nan?"

"Yes, *mon frère*. It is kind of da bomb."

Instead of waiting downstairs, he had run home to drop off his violin.

By late afternoon, we'd been walking and talking and drinking for hours.

I didn't figure on another excursion to the Right Bank

so soon. But that was okay. Andre and I were wending our way all over the 8th while his nonstop Negro-in-Paris history rap unreeled like a guided tour cassette. The kid was amazing.

He had just given me the complete history of the concert hall called the Salle Pleyel, on the rue du Faubourg St. Honoré, where every famous brown person who had ever set foot in Paris—from the players in the old la revue Negre to W.E.B. Du Bois to Herbie Hancock to Howlin Wolf—had drawn an audience.

We stopped briefly for another drink, exchanged more life story tidbits, and pressed on.

It was Andre who pointed out the American Embassy building to me, near the place de la Concorde. But more important to him was the spot a couple of buildings away where once had stood the deluxe club Les Ambassadeurs. I heard all about Florence Mills's success there in 1926 and how Richard Wright had brought Katherine Dunham's dance troupe there to perform in the forties.

As we swept up the Champs Elysées, he listed what Chester Himes and his wife had had for lunch at Fouquet's in 1959. All right, all right—slight exaggeration.

Sidney Bechet this, Henry Tanner that, Kenny Clarke this, Cyrus Colter that . . . Was I aware that *Art Blakey aux Champs-Elysées* was the only live jazz record that . . . Did I want to visit the site of Chez Josephine, la Baker's nightclub, before or after we saw the cabaret where Satie, Milhaud, *and* Ravel used to hang with her . . . In 1961, you know, both Bud and Dexter backed up Carmen McRae at the Paris Blue Note, but it wasn't called that anymore . . .

Who had told this child he wasn't black enough? Not to play amateur Freudian, but his encyclopedic knowledge of our people in Paris was way past the maybe-I'll-write-a-book stage. It was obviously at the level of obsession. Who was he trying to vindicate?

It was late and I was starving. "I'm buying," I told Andre. "What do you suggest?"

"You shouldn't treat," he said. "You've been buying all day."

"It's okay. I'll write it off on my taxes under Educational Expenses."

"You know, there is a place I want to try."

"Name it."

"Bricktop's. It's in the ninth."

He was putting me on. "Oh sure," I said, laughing. "Maybe we'll run into Mabel Mercer and her friend Cole Porter. Scott and Zelda, too." Bricktop, the oh-so-sophisticated cabaret singer, and the club bearing her name were roaring twenties legends, I knew. He had to be putting me on.

"No, no. It's there. Really."

I looked at him then, truly worried. "Jesus. You're really over the edge. I mean, you think we've been transported back to 1928, don't you? I understood that Bricktop's closed about sixty years ago."

He grinned mischievously at me. "Yes, you're right. It did. But there's a place with the same name now. I'd like to see what it's like."

"That's better," I said. "I guess we won't have to get the net for you after all. Are we dressed for it?"

"I think we're cool. It's just a place with down-home food and a piano player."

* * *

Back to funky Pigalle. I had crisscrossed most of these streets before, in my scattershot search for Vivian. Well, this time I wasn't sitting around in the lobbies of grunge hotels, searching for down-and-out bars or the Parisian equivalent to a soup kitchen. I was being escorted around the hallowed grounds of our ancestors, so to speak. The hotel where Bud Powell lived. The cabaret (at least the address where once there had been a cabaret) where one celebrated musician reportedly shot another to death. And, of course, the site of the original Bricktop's on the rue Fontaine.

I felt a flash of guilt about having taken the day off like this. That would be old Ernestine trying to shame me: Vivian's suffering! she was reminding me. Vivian's lost—broke—Vivian's dying! And here you are, drinking the day away *with some man*, chasing after some phantom of the glamorous black past.

Yes, ma'am, I answered meekly. I *am* having too much fun and he *is* too good-looking. Tomorrow I widen the search for Aunt Viv. I swear.

Cole Porter and Mabel Mercer were definitely not in residence. No ladies in bare-back evening gowns and diamonds. Not a tuxedo in sight. The new Bricktop's was African-American kitsch. Autographed photos of the namesake lady herself, of Louis Armstrong and Lady Day, Alberta Hunter and you name them. Stuffed piccaninny dolls. Posters for Oscar Micheaux movies. Laminated Bessie Smith records. Items on the menu named after this or that famous personage. The food wasn't half bad, though. We devoured hot cornbread and smothered chicken and collards while we goofed on the place. The

generic old black gentleman at the baby grand played terrific stride.

They were doing a fairly brisk business in the place,
too. Mostly older black people occupied the tables, but
quite a few younger couples—black, white, black and
white—were chowing down as well. Some musician
types were drinking and bullshitting with the bartender
up front.

A loquacious elderly gentleman we took to be the
owner, because of the deference being paid him by what
appeared to be the regulars, was holding court at a large
round table near the back. The drinks were flowing back
there and spirits were high. One woman at his table we
recognized as an up-and-coming diva from the States—
you know, in one meteoric arc she goes from the church
choir in Stomach Ache, Mississippi, to rave reviews at
the Met. When Andre kept glancing over there, I assumed
it was Miss Thing that he was staring at.

But no, he said, he was looking at the old man. There
was something about him—something vaguely familiar—that he couldn't quite put his finger on.

"He was probably Eubie Blake's butler or something—somebody only you would know," I said mock-
ingly.

He blushed. At least he had enough perspective to be
embarrassed.

I called for the check.

What a day it had been. We began the long walk back
to the 5th, still talking, confiding in each other the way
you do in the early stages of a friendship. Occasionally
I'd point out a café or a restaurant or a street corner where

I'd dined with friends, met a lover, made a discovery of one sort or another.

Back at last at the hotel, we were reluctant to say good night. I invited Andre up for a glass of the brandy I'd been smart enough to purchase and lay away in the armoire.

We set our chairs in front of the open window and went on talking. It wasn't long before a weird kind of chill went up my back. I knew it wasn't from the night air. It was a bizarre sensation and I managed to push it away quickly enough, but I had become somewhat distracted.

"I think I got it!" Andre exclaimed, seemingly out of the blue.

It was as if his voice were coming at me from the bottom of a well. "What? What did you say?"

I had been staring, transfixed, over at the top of the bureau.

"You know that old man—the one who owns Bricktop's?"

"Yeah. What about him?"

"Didn't someone call him Mr. Melson—or Melons?"

"I may have heard somebody call him something like that. Why?"

"I think I know who he is."

"Who?"

"Morris Melon. That's it. He was a teacher. Anthropology, wasn't it? Or sociology. Yes, right. He wrote a book—one of those pioneering studies about the black community in Chicago. Or am I thinking of *Black Metropolis?* It was something like that, anyway. Damn, what was the name of that book? Or was it the study of the

Gullah Islands? I should interview him sometime. Find out his story."

He went on chattering. I was only half listening. I got up and began to walk around the room slowly, a sense of fear rising steadily inside me.

Andre had pulled himself out of his compulsive trip down memory lane. "What's the matter, Nan? What are you doing?"

I began to open the bureau drawers then, checking, I'm not sure what for. I looked inside my sax case and all seemed well there. I could find nothing missing. But I knew that someone had been looking through my things. I just knew it: earrings placed at the right-hand corner of the bureau instead of the left; a tube of hand lotion set on its side rather than on end; pantyhose rolled up with the toes outside rather than in. But things disturbed so minutely that it was possible I was imagining the changes. I told Andre what I was thinking. Moreover, I said, I think it might have something to do with my aunt.

"What do you mean? It was probably just the maid."

I shook my head. "No. No, something's . . ."

"What? What were you going to say?"

"Something's happening."

"Like what? What's happening?"

I had to shrug my shoulders. I had no idea what I meant.

He smiled at me and got me settled down again, almost convinced me that it was my imagination. I sat back at the window with him and finished my drink, but that weird feeling never went completely away.

"I'd better go," Andre said a while later, his voice low. "You need to get to bed."

I nodded. "So do you, friend."

He nodded, too.

A darkness moved across his face then. I didn't understand it. We stood for a minute in the doorway, saying a final good night, and then he left.

Seconds later, there was a knock at the door. He had come back.

"Forget something?" I asked.

"No. Look—uh . . ."

I waited in silence. The darkening in his face was full-blown midnight by now. Something was very wrong.

He dropped the bomb then:

"You think I'm a fag, don't you?"

"Of course not." Oh yes, I did.

I hadn't known it before, but of course I did. What else could it mean for a handsome young man to be staying *chez* "one of my profs."

"I'm not," he said, threatening. He reached for my wrist but at the last moment pulled back. "I'm not gay."

I caught my breath. I didn't speak. He was looking at me so intently that I lowered my gaze from his.

"I'll come over to have breakfast with you tomorrow—if that's okay," he said finally. "We have to do something about your aunt."

We have to do something?

I nodded. "See you in the morning."

Okay, so maybe he wasn't a closet case. But surely there was more to his life story than brilliantly gifted mixed-race kid fights his way out of the ghetto and becomes the toast of Gay Paree. It wasn't that I suspected what he had told me was untrue; there simply had to be some juicy bits that he'd left out.

We.

When he was gone I locked the door and placed my grip in front of it.

CHAPTER 4

It Could Happen to You

I was showered and in street clothes when he arrived.

He was carrying a white box tied with string.

"Coffee's on the way up," I said. "What's that?"

"Decent croissants," he answered, "and sliced ham and some fresh fruit. I stopped at the market near my place." He lifted the sack in his other hand. "And the morning paper."

He laid out all the items on the bureau. "This is the kind of stuff even I can afford," he said.

"Don't worry, boyfriend," I said. "You're going to be rich and famous soon enough."

Thank God, last night's heaviness seemed to have gone from his face, and from the air between us. The tray was delivered a minute later. He sat next to me on the bed and we breakfasted royally.

I felt good, happy, so much less alone.

Unfortunately, when I looked down at the headline

under the fold of the morning paper, that warm and fuzzy feeling instantly went away.

AMERICAN WOMAN BRUTALLY MURDERED

My heart stopped beating for a moment.

Andre noticed the headline a second after I did. We began to read frantically, looking for the name of the victim.

Polk. Mary Polk. A white woman.

I could breathe again.

For about two horrible minutes, I had been absolutely convinced that it was Vivian who had been murdered. But now it was just another story in the news. We read on.

The woman had been bludgeoned to death in the alleyway out back of Le Domino, a seedy bar in Pigalle. She was apparently in France on business, working for a wine wholesaler. She had been registered at a perfectly respectable hotel in the 1st, and was probably indulging some wish to see the wicked side of Paris after dark.

The article went on to say that another patron of the club, one Guillaume Lacroix, had been detained for questioning but already released. The police said Lacroix (street name Gigi) was a petty thief and one-time pimp with a long record, but there was no evidence linking him to the dead woman. The continuation page of the story showed a mug shot of Lacroix looking like a freeze-dried trout.

Another possible suspect, unnamed, was being sought. Authorities believed for now that robbery was the motive for the murder: all Mary Polk's cash, jewelry, and credit cards were taken.

In the gruesome crime scene photo Mary Polk lay dead, a bloody tarpaulin over her upper body, exposed from the knees down. There was something lurid, and at the same time touching, about her shapely ankles in the high heels. Also pictured was the murder weapon—a paperweight wrapped in a "blood-soaked kerchief, olive green in color and with a red insignia sewn on the upper left corner," the news account said.

Sipping at my coffee, I put the paper aside for a minute. Andre picked it up and continued to read, narrating the rest of the story to me as he did so.

I was still thinking about my aunt Vivian. Vivian in her disco-going, coke-snorting, party-animal heyday. I had always admired the way she put herself together—stark black, tight-fitting dresses or bell-bottomed jumpsuits in startling colors. She would scour the flea markets for antique hats and jewelry and shoes. And she almost always wore a scarf. Not a flowing chiffon number, but something more like a cowboy bandanna—a kerchief. She said it added just the right element of fun to her outfits, kind of a throwaway. There was one sort she was especially fond of. A Girl Scout kerchief. Her waist was so tiny she could wear one of those as a sash. In fact, she collected them. She must have had a half dozen of those bandannas.

I grabbed the newspaper from Andre's hands and stared hard at the bloody scarf wrapped around the lethal paperweight. Of course, it was impossible to make out any details in a photo like that, but—No. No, it was crazy. What I was thinking was crazy. It couldn't be. It couldn't.

I jumped off the bed, startling Andre.

"Where are you going?"

"I must be the stupidest cow who ever lived," I said, jamming my feet into my boots.

"What are you talking about? Nan, where are you going?"

"Reception!" I shouted, fumbling with the door. "I'm going to get her suitcase! I should have looked in her suitcase!"

Her valise was humongous. I dragged it onto the birdcage elevator, off again, and into my room.

The case, an old one, was not locked. We hefted it onto the bed and unsnapped the fasteners. It had been packed tight as a drum. All manner of stuff sprang out and onto the coverlet—sweaters, trousers, pantyhose, shampoo—even a photo album.

"I wonder how long she intended to stay," said Andre. "There's a lot of crap in here."

"Yeah," I said, "you're right. And look at the kind of crap it is—I mean, the variety of crap."

There was an impressive panoply of stuff: hair curlers, an old matchbook from the Brasserie Lipp, a portable radio, light clothes, heavy clothes, a couple of mateless earrings, photographs, an empty perfume bottle. A lot of the things seemed more like mementos than travel necessities.

"You know what?" I said. "It's like she grabbed the minimum stuff a person would need to set up housekeeping. Almost like she was going to start a new life."

"She wasn't planning to go home, you mean."

"Maybe. The strangest thing of all is why she would leave it all behind."

"But you said she skipped on the bill."

"Yeah, I know. But if you're deliberately going to skip on the bill, wouldn't you find a way to take a few things out, you know, one at a time in a shopping bag on your way out one morning and nobody would think anything of it. If you were really planning to escape without paying the weekly rent, you'd smuggle your clothes out somehow and just leave the empty suitcase—or something.

"This makes it seem like she left here on the run. Like she hadn't planned to skip at all."

"Could be," he said, picking up the hefty photo album. "Do you remember this?"

"No. I hadn't seen her for a long time. I don't know what kind of things she would have kept at home—wherever that was."

We opened the cover of the album to the first page of photographs.

"That's my grandmother!"

In truth, I had never met my father's mother. She died young. But I recall this photograph of her; my father had a copy of it that used to adorn the chest of drawers in my parents' bedroom.

"God, how strange," I said. "It's so weird seeing that picture again after all these years."

Andre leafed slowly through the book. "He looks like you. Is that your father?" He was pointing to a tall, serious-looking young man in cap and gown.

"Yeah. He looks like he'd rather be someplace else, doesn't he? Like always."

"You don't get along with him?"

"I don't know if I'd put it that way. I don't see him often enough to get along or not get along with him. I was never really sure how Pop felt about me. I was grown up when he left, but it was almost as if when he stopped loving my mother he stopped loving me, too."

"I don't believe it works like that," he said, lingering another minute before he turned the page. "Wow—is that *you?*"

"Where?"

The little girl in pigtails was wearing a polka-dot playsuit, grinning at the camera.

Lord, what a geek I was. I took control of the album and turned hurriedly past the next page or two lest we encounter any shots of me accepting spelling bee or good citizenship prizes.

"There's Vivian!" I cried.

She was wearing a white suit and matching pumps, and a bridal veil. A black man I did not recognize was the groom.

"She's beautiful," Andre said. "Who's the man?"

"Uncle number one, I suppose. She's awful young there. I don't remember him."

"Look here," said Andre. "Looks like another wedding."

Yes, it did. I instantly recognized City Hall in Lower Manhattan. Viv, in a scalloped-neck sheath, her hair teased to giddy heights, and a devilishly handsome man—with an Afro as big as the Ritz—holding up a copy of their marriage license on the steps of the courthouse. Him, I had a vague memory of.

We continued to turn the pages.

Hubby #3 looked familiar, too. Jerry, that's what he was called. "The Cracker," I believe, was my father's pet name for him. Jerry was a musician from L.A. By the look of things, he and Viv had gone to Venice on their honeymoon. And here they were in swim clothes, on a hotel balcony, the Adriatic like a chip of sapphire behind them.

We saw Viv in one of those jumpsuits at a table in some bar. A second-level Motown crooner from the sixties was pawing her. Andre put a name to the guy's face: Chuck Wilson.

There she was again, in a colorful African hat, receiving an autograph from a nice-looking black man, the chairs and tables of a cabaret visible in the background. "That's Oscar Brown Jr.," Andre pronounced.

"You know, I think you're right," I said. "Who's this?" I pointed to the gentleman in another photo, seated at a Steinway, who was shaking hands with Vivian.

"I believe it's Wynton Kelly."

"You're kidding."

"No."

"And what about her?" I said, turning to a snap of Viv in her black evening finery, wineglass raised in salute to a sleepy-eyed lady, also at the piano of some boîte. I slipped the photo out of its cellophane jacket and turned it over, cupping it with my hand so that he could not see what was written there: "Shirley Horn at the Blue Note, 1971."

"Shirley Horn," said Andre.

"Boy, you are fucking amazing. Who's this handsome guy—playing the bass?"

"Ray Brown."

Again, I took the snapshot out and looked at the back of it. He was right again. "Damn, you're good," I said.

He shrugged, trying to hide his swelling chest.

I took out another one and looked at it front and back. "I'm going to stump you on this one, I bet."

"Why?" asked Andre. "Let's see it."

This time I handed the photograph to him. Vivian was pictured with a sweet-faced black man no taller than she was, but beautifully built. They stood with their arms around each other's waist under a sign that read in French EXOTIC GARDEN—THIS WAY.

He studied the man's face for a long time. "Well, I guess you got me," he admitted. "I can't identify him. Let's see who it is." He turned the photo over.

"Picnic With Ez, near Èze! (Ha ha)" was written on the back.

"What does it mean?" Andre asked. "Where is Èze?"

"On the Riviera. We'll have dinner and make a night of it in this incredible hotel someday. When we've got two thousand dollars to blow."

"You mean you've been there?"

"Uh-huh. Once."

"Who took you?"

I gave him a little world-weary sigh. "Oh, you know. Jekyll and Hyde shit. A mistake wearing pants."

"He hit you or something?"

" 'Something.' Yeah, it was more like 'something.' That's the trouble with guys who know a lot more than you: they know *a lot* more than you. Anyhow, I guess I come by my occasional bad taste in men honestly. God knows, Viv had her lapses, too."

He looked down at the snapshot again. "So maybe this guy Ez turned out to be one of Vivian's mistakes. But you say you don't know him?"

I shook my head. "Never heard of him."

We played the game for a few minutes more and then I dived back into the suitcase. More crap, as Andre had called it. But nothing to lead us any closer to Viv. No address books, no airline tickets, no names or phone numbers jotted down on paper napkins. And no Girl Scout bandannas. I guess Viv's waistline wasn't what it used to be.

Finally I came across a fraying denim jacket. I stood up and tried it on. A couple of sizes too small for me and my friends up top. I stuck my hand in one of the chest pockets and pulled out a filthy piece of paper, rolled up tightly like a reefer. I unrolled it. It was, to my astonishment, a hundred dollar bill, U.S. currency.

Andre and I began a thorough search, turning pockets inside out, feeling along seams, opening jars, and so on, but we could find no more cash.

"This was her emergency money, I guess," I said.

"Yeah," he said. "And from what you told me—her telegram to your mother and everything—she had a real emergency. Why didn't she spend it?"

It was a good question.

I put the money back and closed the case, sitting on the lid to get it refastened.

"Know what I think?" I said. "I think Viv left her room one day, just like always, and something happened to her on the outside. I don't know—she saw something or somebody who scared the shit out of her or grabbed her or . . . whatever.

"Either that, or she came back here to the hotel once and found somebody or something waiting for her, and she was too spooked to even come up and get her stuff."

I waited a few seconds, and when he didn't reply, I asked, "Doesn't that sound logical to you?"

This time it was Andre who made a sudden move. All at once he was clearing up the debris from our breakfast and opening the armoire where I kept my things and flinging open the drawers.

"What are you doing that for?"

"Get your stuff," he said. "We're getting out of here. You're leaving this hotel."

"And going where?"

"To my place."

"Why?"

He didn't answer.

"Why?" I asked again. "You think something's going to happen to me here. Is that what you're saying?"

"I don't know. But I think you should leave. You could save the money, in any case."

"You believe somebody was here last night now—is that it?"

"No—I mean, I don't know—it's possible. But aside from all that, I want you to come. I want you to stay with me."

I called downstairs and told them I would be checking out and that I'd need to retrieve the envelope I'd stashed in the safe.

"You know, Andre," I said when I had finished packing, "I bonded like this—with a strange man—once before. Only once."

"What happened?"

"Not good. Not good. It ended up terrible."

CHAPTER 5

Straight Street

I sprang from the cab.

"Holy shit. You live on the rue Christine?!"

"Yeah," he said. "Didn't I mention it?"

"You most certainly did not, Andre."

"You're tripping because you know Baldwin once lived on this street. Is that it?"

"No, fool. I'm 'tripping' because I love this goddamn street like a schoolboy loves his cherry pie. When you said you got the ham in the market, you meant the market at rue de Buci, didn't you?"

He answered, but I wasn't even listening.

I was running up the stairs ahead of him.

"What floor?" I called down to him while he struggled with Viv's suitcase.

"Top."

Holy shit!

The tea shop across the street, with the madeleines to

die for. The blind man in the fountain pen shop. The fifty-seat cinema at the end of the block. There was a time when I'd have become a common prostitute to live on this block, sold my grandmother, given away my soul. I had been walking on the street perpendicular to this one, rue de Seine, one summer afternoon—I was nineteen years old—and I'd turned down this street and opened my arms to it. I couldn't even have told you why; there were far more beautiful places to live right in this neighborhood. But I had returned to this street again and again, walked it at all times of the day and night, observing the life that went on, pretending I lived in the apartment over the lingerie store. I used to see this street in my dreams after I'd returned to school that fall.

And now Andre was turning the key in the lock and letting me into—holy shit! A skylight. The apartment was tiny, but so beautiful. Was this really happening? I was flying around that room, touching everything—the lamp, the kitchen sink, the stereo.

I turned to face Andre, who was regarding me as if I were insane. I suddenly began to laugh helplessly. No wonder he thought I was nuts. I was acting like—like a schoolgirl version of Andre, when he had some Negro arcana in his teeth.

By the time my fit of laughter was over, his expression had changed. I knew that face: desire. Wrong word. Desire was the least of it. His face read, as clearly as the headline in the morning paper, You are going to be fucked. No preliminaries. No talk. For better or worse. Fucked.

I didn't contradict it, I didn't examine it. I was too busy tearing out of my dress.

I ran—ran—to my valise and tried to claw it open, looking for a condom. But he overpowered me, pinned me where I stood. I stopped struggling, fearing he would snap my windpipe with the strong hand at my neck. Fearing, period. I was afraid of him, but even more afraid of the brute strength of my own desire, which had me grunting like a half-wit as we fell to the rug with him tearing at my underpants.

He was on me. Everywhere. Prying me open. Sucking. Thrusting inside me like a wild boar. Crying out. With my nail, I had accidentally opened a small gash over his left eyebrow. We were either going to come together or kill each other.

There was unbearable grief in his throat when he finished. I dug my fingers into his hair, pulled his head up off my breast momentarily and looked into his eyes. His face was pasty and wet and he was sobbing. I covered his mouth with mine and we rolled over and lamely began to fuck again.

Through his tears he spoke for the first time since we had entered the room. What he said was, "Belong to me."

"I do," I said, not missing a beat.

He made coffee with his back to me. Nothing on except his shorts. That wonderful barely there butt of his seemed to wink at me like a pornographic sign. A warming breath blew across my desire, heating me up again. Inside my head, I went to the next time I would lie gasping under him, barely able to lift myself to him; the next time I'd lick at the sweat in the hollow of his neck in syncopation with the stroking of his finger inside me. Greedy

Nan, greedy girl. I pushed the image aside, busied myself with unpacking.

He got the windows open, then poured coffee and brought mine over to me in a small yellow cup.

"Nan?"

I looked up at him.

"I have never done anything like that before," he said. "Not even close."

"Neither have I," I said, "and I'm a slut. By some standards, I mean."

The next forty-eight hours went by in a blur. I know I phoned Mom to tell her I'd—ahem—changed residences and to give her a no-progress progress report. I know Andre and I had two or three quick meals in the café across the street from the apartment. I know we made a couple of scouting excursions to low-down hotels and hostels to inquire about Vivian, and in desperation we did place an ad in the *Trib*. But mostly those two days, those hours, went by in a haze of the headiest, funkiest, sexiest sex I had ever taken part in.

The caveman-type coupling gradually faded into long looks and longer kisses and driving each other wild with touches and tongues, and doing it in the bathtub, and feeding each other cheese with our fingers, and generally going through each other like two kids with a box of cookies.

It was damn hard to keep my mind on Aunt Viv and her troubles. But on the third day the fog began to lift and I was able to focus a little better.

Andre and I went back to the hotel on Cardinal Lemoine that afternoon, just on the chance that Vivian had come back to pay her bill and collect her things. No such luck on that score. But the madame, to whom we presented a staggering bouquet of flowers, was good enough to conduct another phone search for us: this time to determine whether Vivian was in jail under any of her various names.

Andre and I were still unable to keep our hands off each other, but we had at least come back to earth sufficiently to be hungry for a homemade meal. On the way back to the apartment we stopped to acquire groceries and wine in the open-air market. I put the chicken in the small oven and set about peeling some potatoes. While I worked, he supplied a beautiful serenade—a medley of standards that sounded utterly fresh and even downright foreign on the violin.

After dinner the concert resumed. I was eating his "Don't Worry 'Bout Me" with a spoon, when he stopped mid-note, the queerest look on his face.

"What?" I said, pulling myself out of the reverie.

"I just got the greatest idea."

Wasn't it wonderful, my beloved had an idea.

"What idea?"

"You know 'Sentimental Mood,' don't you?"

"Sure," I said.

"Okay. And—let's see—what else? Do you know 'Blue Room'?"

"Of course."

"Go get your sax."

Duets!

Why the hell not? Talk about your peas in a pod. Two jazz-drunk African-American neo-francophiles.

I'd never given much thought to jazz violinists before

I met Andre. Now I kicked myself for not making an effort to see artists like Regina Carter or Maxine Roach and the all-female group she was involved in back in New York: the Uptown String Quartet.

I was now of the opinion that violinists made the perfect musical colleagues. Stuff Smith had collaborated most successfully with Dizzy, and with Nat Cole and Ella. Who else? Joe Venuti, of course. Then there was the old gentleman they called "Fiddler"—Claude Williams, who, if he only had four arms, could accompany himself on the guitar. And, almost too obvious to mention: the Grappelli-Reinhardt combination.

The world thought I was just little old me from Queens. Ha! Little did they know, I was Django's illegitimate gypsy granddaughter.

CHAPTER 6

Lush Life

It was time for a bold move.

Time was flying away from me. Before Vivian became nothing more than a memory, I had to do something forceful, something concrete. And I had to do it now.

That is why I made the decision to dip into the murky end of the pool, going once again to Pigalle.

As far as we knew, Vivian wasn't dead or dying. But that didn't mean she wasn't still in trouble. The way I saw it, if she was indigent, hungry, unable to go back to the hotel for her money, and surely unable to get any kind of job over here, she might well have turned to something not so legit, if not outright felonious. And so I decided to seek help from the only French criminal I knew—make that *knew of*.

The first bold step I took was to tell a whopping big lie to Andre. I said that I'd run into an old classmate in the drugstore. She was living in Paris and she and I were going to get together for a night of drinking, roasting men, and catching up. It was to be girls-only, I told him; next time we got together, I'd ask him to join us.

See, I knew he would go nuts if I told him what I was really planning to do. So he spent the evening playing with a couple of other musicians way out in Passy, while I joined my mythical girlfriend for dinner.

The newspaper accounts of the murder of Mary Polk, the American businesswoman, had made Le Domino, the club where she was killed, sound like sin central. But in fact it was sort of like the French version of the dive where my friend Aubrey danced in New York. A lot of drunks. A few ambulatory junkies. Watery booze and skinny whores and a bunch of randy men who ought to know better.

I chatted up the bartender and tipped outrageously and hung around long enough drinking donkey-piss beer to get my reward: Gigi Lacroix, the ex-pimp who had been questioned and released in the Mary Polk investigation, put in an appearance about one A.M.

Yeah, he was a bit oily. But I had been prepared for that. I didn't expect a guy in a beret carrying a marked-up copy of *Nausea* or humming Jacques Brel's greatest hits. I predicted a certain sleaze factor and I got it. Gigi was a thin fellow with a thin mustache, a bad haircut, and a line of bullshit as long as a summer day in Stockholm.

The thing was, with his big Charles Aznavour eyes and Popeye swagger, he was kind of adorable along with it.

Gigi said he had not run a stable of hookers in more than ten years; "that nonsense" was all in the past. To hear him tell it, he was an old coot now—enjoying his retirement, and for all he knew, "looking up the ass of death." Guillaume Lacroix claimed he was now just a regular *mec* who liked his dinner hot and on time, and of course a glass of wine now and then. *But* . . . if a nice man was in dire need of female companionship, or if one person with something to sell needed an introduction to another person with the wish to buy? He broke off with that emblematic Gallic shrug. *"Entendu?"*

Understand? Sure I did, I said, managing to slide my hand out of his grip and signal the bartender for another round.

Unlike a lot of his stuffy countrymen, Gigi adored Americans, he assured me. Especially Al Pacino. Did I love the movies as much as he did?

Oh, absolutely.

Was I, or this fellow I was traveling with, involved in any way with the film industry?

Sadly, no, I had to admit, but we were both musicians—did that count for anything?

"Not really," said Gigi. "Paris is lousy with musicians—no offense." In any case, he said, he wasn't the one to talk music with. His lady friend Martine was the music expert. She'd probably be dropping in around two-thirty.

I saw no reason to fence with Gigi Lacroix. He was no more a cop lover than I was. I laid out the Aunt Viv story for him. Let's say it was the edited version of the Viv story. Leaving out any mention of the ten grand I was going to give her, I stressed how worried the family was about her; I was on a mission, out to rescue my adventurous aunt, who drank a little and who'd always had more nerve than brains.

While Gigi listened he casually downed another in the army of Pernods I was paying for.

"Hmph," he uttered at the end of the tale. "I don't know the lady. She sounds like an exciting woman, though."

"Do you think you could help me? Do some asking around?"

There went another defining gesture: the puffed-out lips accompanied by raised eyebrows and a slant of the head. Maurice Chevalier in polyester. The guy cracked me up.

I figured we could come to terms.

"*Écoute*, Gigi," I said, "you're not going to be able to retire to the mountains on what I can pay you, but I think we can work something out. There's just one thing I've got to get straight."

"Of course," he said expansively.

"Did you have anything to do with Mary Polk's death?"

The false bonhomie fell away from his face then and he shook his head once. "The unfortunate victim," he said, "was another lady I never had the pleasure of meeting. We simply happened to be in the wrong place at the wrong time—both of us."

I had a sudden image of that Girl Scout bandanna. It just flew in and out of my thoughts. "Did you get a look at the death scene? Out back I mean, where the police found her?"

"Me? No, my friend. I'm no ghoul. I have no curiosity about the dead. Especially when the police are involved."

I took that in without comment.

It was a bit like the time I found my dream chair on

sale at a furniture outlet store back in New York. The price was unbelievably low. I couldn't find a thing wrong with it, and I knew that if it turned out to have been put together with spit, I'd never get my money back. I knew, furthermore, the salesman was the last person I should look to for reassurance. Yet I did. I also told him that at the first sign of a hidden defect, I'd come back there and get postal on his ass. I had absolutely no means of backing up that threat. But he took me at my word, and I left the store with his personal unconditional guarantee in hand. One of those rare occasions when racism works for you rather than against you.

So it was that I threw in with Gigi the aging pomaded pimp—with the promise that if he tried to fuck me over he'd have to call in Al Pacino to get me off his case. I'd make his retirement uncomfortable as hell, even report to the police that he'd told me he knew who killed Mary Polk as well as my aunt.

Did he take my threats seriously? Not very, I wagered. But I decided to go with him anyway.

It was while he was comparing *Godfather III* to the other installments in the saga that Martine walked in. Gigi Lacroix was like a thousand other trifling guys I'd seen in the world: unregenerate larceny in his heart, living off the weaknesses of others, quick-witted, shrewd, and lazy. When all was said and done, a colorful underworld character, no more. His lady friend Martine, on the other hand, scared the bejesus out of me.

For starters, my girl had a *scar*—jawbone to neck. No taller or more powerfully built than he, but there was menace in her very walk. She locked glances with Gigi, ignoring me utterly until he introduced us, at which time she swept her burning eyes across my face and torso. I looked down at her stiletto-heeled shoes, which consisted entirely of straps and laces that crawled up her ankles like garter snakes.

Martine seemed to take up all the space at the bar. She and Gigi went into a wanton lovers' clutch for a couple of minutes and then he ran down my story for her. She took it in without comment, helping herself to a belt of Gigi's Pernod.

It was after 4 A.M. when I got back to the rue Christine apartment. Andre was sleeping peacefully, waking only long enough to ask if I'd had a good time with my fictitious chum—and he wasn't one of the guys we roasted, was he?

No way, I said, and pressed his head back onto the pillow. Then I went in to shower the stale tobacco and barroom funk out of my pores.

When we got up the next morning, I'd have to tell him the truth about the evening and prepare him for Gigi.

As predicted, he was not amused. I saw the worst of his play-it-safe side as he turned into my father for fifteen minutes. He blasted me for my foolishness in going into that den of iniquity; preached at me for jeopardizing our status as nice colored foreigners; ridiculed my private-eye fantasies, and so on.

I sat there and took it, goddammit. But, under my patient, reasoned, point-by-point defense, he had to agree in the end that playing it safe was getting us nowhere with the Vivian quest.

Once we had a late breakfast and hit the streets, he continued to punish me for a couple of hours with all the quick-step melodies he could think of. I was hung over, but I'd be damned if I wouldn't keep up with him.

The folks at the outdoor tables loved our ass. They were giving us an overwhelming round of applause. Andre's violin case was stuffed with francs. We had played duets all over Paris, and this was one of our favorite spots. We made just as much or more here as at Au Père Tranquille or the gargantuan café on rue St. Denis, where the hookers sometimes helped us with our pitch, or playing for hours in the métro.

"Could you *play* any faster than that?" I said through my teeth.

"Stop being sarcastic and concentrate," he said. There was that smirk again. I wanted to slap him.

Not really true. Number one: whenever I looked at that mouth of his, smirking, smiling, whatever, all I wanted to do was die in his arms. Number two: he had done the impossible—flogged me, metaphorically that is, until I learned to play Bird's "Segment" at the proper breakneck speed. How could I be mad at him? Andre believed I was a better musician than I did, and whether he was right or wrong, I had, beyond question, improved immensely. I could feel it happening, evolving, every day I spent with him. It was as if I were topping myself in a cutting contest with me.

"We're knocking off now—right?" I threatened, already packing up. Little or no sleep last night, I was exhausted.

"Yeah, right," he said. "Let's go home."

He put an arm around me and together we tripped across the avenue de la Grande Armée in the kind spring air. Through the traffic, across the noisy boulevards and the narrow streets we went, not talking at all. We were heading back to the apartment to clean ourselves up, and inevitably to make love, before going to meet Gigi for dinner. Life was so good it almost scared me.

Almost. There was no need yet to feel the gods were about to lower the boom on my perfect life. Because of course life wasn't perfect. I had not found Vivian. Indeed, I had not come within a mile of finding her—not a single lead—and it was starting to eat me up inside. I'd be happy if Gigi turned up even the slightest little piece of information.

Back in the safety of the little love nest on rue Christine, I took a nice nap in the afterglow of afternoon sex. Odd how afternoon dreams are the worst, but afternoon fucking is usually the best.

Around seven that evening Andre and I pulled into virtually matching outfits: black jeans and white shirts. Each checking the other out and gaining assurance that we looked really cool, we left the apartment and caught the métro at St. Michel, heading for the bistro in the Bastille where Gigi liked to eat.

The place sure had the right smell. Onion and rosemary, rabbit and scallops, sweetbreads and hundred-year-old cheese and rich red wine danced around my senses. I searched the noisy, plain room for Gigi, but he had not yet arrived. We took a table, the burner under my appetite suddenly cranked up to red alert. Andre and I were devouring olives when I caught sight of Monsieur Lacroix, the lovely Mamselle Martine in tow.

We had a sensational meal. And I bet there wasn't another foursome like us in the place: Gigi and I doing most of the talking as he reported on the people he'd asked about Aunt Vivian; Andre looking a little uncomfortable but gamely trying out his newly mastered French idioms on Gigi; and Martine, who clearly thought Gigi's mission was preposterous, barely speaking at all but commanding and drinking wine as though—well, as though she was paying for it.

"We are fairly sure your aunt is not in the life," Gigi pronounced.

Well, that was nice to hear. Aunt Viv, as far as Gigi could determine, was not currently a streetwalker. I stole a quick glance at Martine, who was guffawing.

Martine seemed as eager to show off her rather good English as Andre was to master colloquial French. "So what is this story?" she said expansively, helping herself to more wine, "the two of you are playing what? That . . . *jazz?*" She formed the word as if it were something gross she had come upon in the refrigerator.

"That's right," I said. "What's the matter? Don't you like jazz?"

She shrugged. "It is useless. Anyone can play popular music."

"Oh really?" I said mildly. *Oh really? Is that so, you charmless whore?* "What sort of music do you admire, Martine?"

"Ze blues," she answered immediately.

Andre and I exchanged looks. I had to admit, his was more amused than mine.

"People are always speaking about these jazz men," Martine said dismissively. "How brilliant they are, how sophisticated. I say 'shit' to sophistication. The only real American music is the blues. Can you and your man with his silly little girl's pigtails do what John Lee Hooker does? (*Jean Lee Ook-heir*, she pronounced it actually.) Do you have his pain? Do you have his *cri de coeur*? Or Lightning Hopkins (*Op-keens*)? No! You can play your childish ballads all you want, but you will never make anyone feel the way Muddy Waters did. No. You *have* no feeling compared to them. No soul. I do not care how black you are."

What could I do? If I got up and bitch-slapped her, which was what she deserved, it was going to cause no end of trouble. Somebody might panic and call for help. Gigi might pull out of the deal and leave me right back where I started. Or, just as likely, Martine, despite the thirty pounds I had on her, might end up kicking the shit out of me. I kept my seat. It had to be the high road for now.

"Well, thank you, Martine," I said crisply. "That was most informative. Tell me, is Muddy Waters your very favorite noble savage?"

"Do not patronize me."

"Patronize *you*?" Andre repeated, not so amused anymore.

She shirked off his remark. "If you are really interested in who I like—for me, there is no one like Haskins. He was the best blues man of them all."

Haskins? Who the hell was that?

I looked to Andre, Mr. Negro Music, for help. But apparently he, too, was drawing a blank on the name.

"It does not surprise me that you have not heard of him," Martine said sniffily. "See, Mr. Pigtails? I told you, you know nothing about the soul."

The three of us—Gigi, the slow-boiling Andre, and I—all sat back as Martine launched into her lecture.

"Little Rube Haskins," she said, "was a giant. A hero. He was unfairly locked up in your racist Mississippi prisons. But he escaped, first to Canada and then to Marseilles. Finally he came to Paris. He was the last in a line of giants like Leadbelly and 'Owling Wolf."

Andre listened intently as she rattled on. "Listen, Martine," he said when at last she stopped for a breather, "are you telling me this Haskins was living and singing in Paris in the 1970s?"

"Yes, that is right."

"And he wrote all these songs himself, you say?"

"That is right."

"But . . . but how come I don't know anything about this genius? I mean, why doesn't his name turn up in anybody's book? Why don't we see him listed as the composer on any folk music? How come I never once even heard the guy's name?"

Martine used Gigi's disposable lighter to fire up her cigarette. She took a luxurious puff from it and then told Andre, "You expect me to explain your ignorance to you? This I cannot do."

Sharp intake of breath. Like he was counting to ten. "I don't suppose you have any of his records?"

"Records!" Martine scoffed. "Records? He had no records. The music industry is interested only in money, not in the truth. Haskins was appreciated only by the aficionados. Besides, just as he was about to go into the studio to make an album—he died."

"So how did you hear him? You went to these places where the aficionados hung out? Or to some kind of underground concerts?"

"What are you talking about, you ignorant man? I

never saw him in my life. How old do you think I am? I was only a girl then. I've heard the tape recordings made of him at the clubs. They're collector's items today."

Andre gave her a lingering look of appraisal, full of skepticism.

Gigi, draining his glass, placed a proprietary arm around Martine's shoulder. "My Martine is like an encyclopedia, you know. Full of information—and opinions—no?"

"Yeah," said Andre, in English. "Full of it."

I gave him a sharp look.

"Hey, Martine," he challenged, "what's your favorite song by this giant—what's-his-name—Rube Haskins?"

" 'The Field Hand's Prayer,' " she snapped right back at him.

"The what?!" He reared back in his chair, openly laughing at her.

This time, the look I threw him had broken glass in it.

"You find it funny?" Martine said, going red at the ears. "You think Haskins could not write a song better than the weak, pitiful white immigrants you jazz musicians worship? You would rather hear something by Cole Porter than the words coming from the heart of the descendant of a slave? What sort of idiot does this make you?"

Oh shit.

To quote my friend Aubrey, *What you have to say that for?*

Andre's eyeballs were orbiting their sockets. Spittle at the corner of his mouth. Fists clenched. All the signs of a man about to go ballistic.

He leaned toward her threateningly. "Listen, you

skank, what you know about the blues—" was all I let him get out before I smashed into his ankle with my low-cut boot.

"Andre!" I called into his face like a drill sergeant. "We'll have Martine over to the apartment for a night of shop talk some other time! We've got plenty of other stuff to talk about right now, don't we, Andre?"

He was fuming, but he shut up and, except for the stray wisecrack, remained that way while I passed a few more hundred francs to Gigi and listened to his rundown of where he was going to go later that night to ask about Vivian's whereabouts. I wrote down the phone number at the rue Christine apartment and he tucked it into his pocket.

Before the party broke up, Martine had an Armagnac and ordered espressos for all. Generous of the cow, wasn't it? I didn't want any goddamn coffee, but she had moved too quickly. I paid the check, glowering at her and at Andre.

We parted from them on the street, Gigi bursting with good manners and good will.

"Stop worrying," he said reassuringly. "I will find your wayward aunt."

"Y'all can stop worrying, too," Andre muttered under his breath. "Why don't you take a fucking cab to the Delta on our money? Check out some authentic blues."

I waited until our dinner companions turned the corner before loosing my rage on my lover.

"Andre, what the fuck do you mean, starting a fight over some lame ass singer with that dumb whore?"

"What the fuck do you mean, *starting*? I didn't start it!

That 'dumb whore' had the nerve to talk to me about slaves!"

"Shut up, fool! You let that silly woman bait you. You let your know-it-all musical ego run away with you—like it was your balls on the line instead of finding Vivian. Finding Vivian! That's the real point here, remember? I wouldn't give a rat's ass for Martine's musical opinions either, but I can't afford to let this guy Gigi go yet. It'd be like flushing my money down the toilet, and we still wouldn't know anything. It's . . . It's . . . God damn, what is the matter with you, Andre!"

Our second public brawl. Screaming at each other— that's how this relationship had started. We went at it full throttle there in front of the restaurant, a few curious on-lookers, non-English-speakers, I guessed, treating it as though we were the evening's entertainment: like we were street theater.

We used the walk home to cool down.

By the time we shut the door of the apartment behind us, I was exhausted all over again. I put on water for herbal tea and grudgingly made enough for Andre as well.

I plopped his cup down in front of him at the table.

"I'm sorry," he mumbled.

I grunted.

"I'm *really* sorry."

That sent me into his lap, tearing up and snuffling. He rocked me for a while.

"I'm trying to do what's right, Andre," I said. "I'm just trying to do right by Auntie Viv. I don't know, maybe I'm just feeling guilty because I used to wish Viv was my mother instead of—instead of my perfectly serviceable lovely mom. Pop treated Viv so bad, you know? Just because she decided she wasn't going to be a housewife in Queens—just because she wasn't all buttoned up and appropriate like him. Because she wanted to be free. I loved her for showing me that. I fucking *owe* her for that. Viv made a lot of stupid moves, but she lived her life—you know? I have to find her, Andre. Not just because of the money—I want to know she's okay."

"I understand," he said, trying to quiet me, wiping at my tears.

"I was awful to you, wasn't I?" I said. "Cussing and carrying on like that."

"Yeah, you're an awful bitch. A real *margère*—a shrew."

"*Mégère*," I corrected him.

"Thank you, teacher. Let's go to bed, let's go to bed, let's go to bed."

I laughed. "So a crying woman gets you hard, huh?"

"A paper clip gets me hard, Nan. I want inside you."

No time to undress. Push the hot tea aside. Straddling him on the little wooden chair. He unbuttons my jeans. Shirt over my face. My arms immobile. Can't see him, what he's doing. Just feel him, working his way in. Poking blindly at his eyes. Fight free of the shirt, buttons popping. Tugging on his braids. He's picking me up. I'm gummy with lust. Irradiated.—"I'm sorry."—"I know."—"I love you."—"I know."—"Don't leave me."—"I won't. Promise to play the Ravel for me, after," I say through a giggle.—"Yes. All right. Oh yes," he says.

Pressed tightly up against my back, he soaped my hair.

"I've got a surprise in store for you," said Andre, straining to be heard over the knocking of the old pipes in the shower stall.

"Ha! That ain't no surprise, Geechee. You get one of those just about every half hour."

"No, not that," he said. "This is something we have to go outside for."

"What? Where?"

"It's on the street."

"What street?"

"I don't know the name of it. We just have to walk till we find it."

"It" turned out to be a dusty, narrow shop near the Comédie Française. It specialized in music scores and art relating to music. The two older women who ran the place nodded warmly—maybe even conspiratorially—to Andre and let us wander undisturbed all over the shop. I was in hog heaven, oohing and aahing over a photo of Billy Strayhorn arm in arm with Lena Horne, when Andre disappeared up the aisle. I could hear him exchanging hushed words with one of the ladies. In a minute the two of them approached me carrying a framed pen-and-ink sketch.

Andre turned it so that I could see it full view.

"Monk!" I screamed.

"*C'est beau, oui?*" the owner said, smiling.

"It's beautiful," I agreed.

"And it's yours," said Andre.

"Mine?" I grabbed it out of his hands. "Really *mines*?"

"Yeah, I bought it—in three installments."

I gave him a dozen kisses.

We were having a great time in there. While the sketch

was being wrapped, I continued to browse. I went up and down the rows, flipping through all kinds of memorabilia and photos. It was in the bargain rack marked "Miscellaneous" that I came across the most startling piece of all.

"Andre!" I shouted out.

They must have thought I'd been bitten by a fat sewer rat or something, because all hands rushed over to where I stood.

"What is it?" he asked in alarm.

"Look at this photograph!" I pointed to a shiny head shot of a pomaded black man trying to look pensive and irresistible. "Look at the caption and tell me if I'm dreaming."

"Jesus Christ," Andre said. Just that.

"Little Rube Haskins," I quoted the caption. "It says this is Martine's hero, Rube Haskins—right?"

"Yeah. It does."

"Man, do you know who this *is*?" I said, my eyes popping. "Take a good look."

"I don't have to," he replied. "That's your aunt Vivian's friend. Ez—from Èze."

CHAPTER 7

Pop!Pop!Pop!Pop!

Not that we had anything much to celebrate, but Andre and I went clubbing that night. Bricktop's.

The joint was jumping.

I had bought that amateur photo of Rube Haskins and we had run home from the music shop to compare it with the one in Vivian's scrapbook. No question about it; my aunt's Riviera companion and the obscure blues genius called Rube Haskins were one and the same man.

Sitting in the apartment, looking in bewilderment from one picture to the other, I got one of those shit! why didn't I think of it before? flashes. The original Bricktop had been a social lion. Everybody who was anybody in jazz-age Paris had passed through her door. Perhaps it was the same kind of thing with the present owner of Bricktop's. He might actually have known Haskins.

"Let's get over there," I urged Andre. We could talk to the owner before we hit the streets to play tonight.

It was one move that Andre had no trouble endorsing. It seemed safe enough to go and talk to Morris Melon. He was no ex-pimp with a razor-scarred girlfriend, and it seemed unlikely he'd make us pay by the hour for a little conversation.

I wriggled into my long, tight brown skirt with a matching sweater cropped so short that its bottom hem fell just below my nipples. I tucked the Rube Haskins head shot into my purse and Andre and I grabbed our respective axes and headed out into the night.

Like I said, the joint was jumping. In fact, the whole town was bustling. After all, it was springtime in Paris. Folks at Bricktop's were finger popping and flirting, eating and drinking with abandon, and gathering around the pianist to request their favorite song.

The elderly proprietor was just as much in the spirit as his customers. Morris Melon was drunk as a lord.

Leaning on his spiffy cane, he was up near the entrance greeting people as they walked in.

Small man, big voice. "Children!" his basso rang out when we stepped across the threshold. *"Bienvenu!"*

"Merci, Monsieur Melon," I said as he waved us to the crowded bar. "Will you allow us to buy you a drink?"

"Lord yes," he agreed, and joined us there.

Andre started out slowly enough, but was soon in high gear with his music and tell-me-about-being-black-in-Paris quiz. We listened attentively while the old man pontificated and reminisced and testified, though I suspect that Andre already knew the answers to most of the questions he posed.

After he had related yet another fascinating anecdote

about his life in Paris—and to be fair, his stories *were* fascinating—we zeroed in on the real target.

"Mr. Melon," I said, "we have a French friend who's wild about a blues singer who used to live in Paris. I'd like to get her some of his records, but I can't find any of them for love nor money. Do you know anything about him? Little Rube Haskins was his name."

He burst into high-pitched, derisive laughter. " 'Rube' is right, *ma chère*. He was right off the boat. What the children in Chicago used to call a country nigger. To paraphrase that Ozark woman's song—a little bit country, a little bit rhythm and blues."

"You mean you actually met him?"

"Once or twice. You know what they say—if you stay in Paris long enough, you meet everyone in the world."

"Did you ever hear him perform?" asked Andre.

Melon rolled his eyes. "Yes, child."

"No good?"

"Good and bad didn't come into it. He was ridiculous. He could play that guitar well enough, I'll give him that, but his songs about his mule jumping over the moon or some such were so derivative and falsely primitive as to be preposterous. None of the sweetness, none of the heart, the grace of the rural Negro—no blessedness. And I should know, child. I'm a proud country nigger myself. I just found the man vulgar, to be candid. But then again . . . oh, I don't know why I'm fussing so much. I suppose he was just trying to enjoy the party, like the rest of us. To be fair, he did have a following here for a hot minute. But he was a footnote to a footnote, at best. I can't imagine that anyone let him make any recordings."

"When did you know him?" I asked. "How long ago?"

"Ah. Well, that's not so easy to say. Fifteen—eighteen—twenty years? Time doesn't mean a great deal to someone like me, you know. Not anymore." He laughed that marvelous deep laugh again and took the fresh martini the barman handed him.

"Might I just show you something?" I said.

"Of course. Show me everything, dear girl."

I retrieved the glossy photograph from my bag and held it close to his hand resting on the bar.

"Is that what he looked like?"

"Have mercy!" he said in wonderment. "Yes, that was him. Don't tell me your friend carries his picture around?"

"Well," I said, "she does adore him. All she's ever heard are a couple of badly recorded tapes of him. She found this in one of the stalls on the Seine."

He turned the photo over in his hands a couple of times. "The French are peculiar, *n'est-ce pas*?" he said philosophically. "Wonderful—but peculiar. And would we have it any other way?"

After a moment's appreciative laughter, Andre asked, "What happened to Haskins, Mr. Melon? We heard he died young."

"Umm. I think that's true. Died young and died tawdry, if I'm remembering it right. Let me see—must have been a drunken brawl somewhere—no—it was a jealous husband—or a woman scorned—something like that. He was shot to death in a car perhaps. Something absurd like that. He didn't have the decency to just choke on a pig's foot."

I couldn't help it: I let out a shriek of laughter.

"Oh, I'm mean, child," Mr. Melon said. "I'm just terrible, ain't I?"

Melon slid smoothly from his barstool, cane and all, when a party of five came barreling in, shouting their greetings at him.

I had to get in just two more quick questions before he took his leave of us.

"By the way," I said, "did you happen to know any of Rube's lady friends? One in particular called Vivian?"

"Oh dear, I don't think so." He pursed his lips then. "The only Vivian I recall from those days was a young man, not a young lady. A British chap, and the less said about him the better."

"Last question," I said. "Any idea if Rube Haskins was his real name? I mean, did you ever hear people call him by any other name?"

He shook his head "Just 'fool.' You two children should have some of that St. Emilion before you leave tonight. It's delicious. Ask Edgar to pour you some."

"He's something, isn't he?" Andre said when Melon was out of earshot.

"He's a stitch. But I wouldn't want him to read me. He's got one sharp tongue."

"What now?"

"Yeah. You got that right. What now? We know for sure now this is Haskins. But where does that leave us? How did he go from Ez to Rube—or vice versa? And which one was he when Vivian went picnicking with him?"

Andre began to speak, but he stopped short when Morris Melon reappeared at the bar.

"Is it true what I hear, children?" he asked us excitedly.

We looked at him blankly.

"That's right, play it coy, babies," he laughed expansively. "Don't be so modest! Some friends tell me you two are the talk of the town. They say *le tout Paris* is buzzing about the duets you've been performing. You must favor us with something."

His slow, steady clapping caught fire and before we knew it the whole restaurant was filled with coaxing applause.

After a brief consult with the pianist, we started with the old Nat Cole arrangement of "Just You, Just Me." A real up number. Everybody seemed to enjoy it. Then the old musician removed himself to a table and left us on our own.

Andre's beauty obligato for me on "Something to Live For" seemed to come out of nowhere. Gorgeous. I was inspired, and tried to return the favor for his solo work on "I Didn't Know About You." Someday you've *got* to hear that on the violin. We closed with "I Didn't Know What Time It Was."

I guess we killed. Applause like thunder. The waiters began to anoint us with complimentary drinks.

Andre and I recaptured our places at the bar and Morris Melon hurried over to clink his glass with mine. "You children are too beautiful to live," he cried in delight. "I want you to promise you'll come and play for us at least once a week."

Andre began to stutter.

"I won't take no for an answer," Melon pressed. "We'll feed you right, offer you our finest wines, and you can put your own tips bowl out on the piano."

Andre and I looked at each other and shrugged. We nodded okay at the old man.

"Babies," he said, grinning, "I couldn't be happier."

If you don't know what boulevard St. Germain looks like at four in the morning as you sit outdoors at the Deux Magots . . . I won't spoil it for you by talking about it.

We had received all those strokes from the fabulous Morris Melon; the street crowds had been supergenerous; we'd stopped at one of my old haunts, an all-night place, for a perfect little meal; I was actually living on rue Christine, my street of dreams; the low sky was showing Paris pink around the edges; and, not least, this beautiful man I was in love with, was in love with me, apparently to the point of stupidity.

Again, heaven seemed almost within my grasp. But I couldn't be happy. I couldn't rest. We were no closer to finding Vivian. She was, if anything, slipping further away.

"You gotta do something for me tomorrow," I said, turning to Andre.

He polished off his almond croissant. "You mean today, don't you, sweetheart?"

"Right. Here's the thing: Vivian knew this guy Rube Haskins."

"Check."

"Only he had a different name."

"Check."

"And he was murdered—maybe over a woman, maybe *by* a woman."

"Check—Wait a minute. You don't think your aunt was the woman—or the woman scorned?"

"The pig's foot, so to speak. Of course I don't know that she had anything to do with it. But at any rate, it had to be in the papers, right? There has to be some kind of investigation when anybody gets murdered. And Haskins was a public figure, even if he was a really minor celebrity—Mister Footnote. We have to find out if the police ever got the whole story. If they arrested anybody. Maybe somebody from his family came over here to claim the body. Maybe Vivian's name turns up as just someone the cops contacted for information."

"Maybe," he said. "So what is it you want me to do?"

"The murder happened, what, almost twenty-five years ago. I'm going to make a run to the library tomorrow, and make a phone call or two to some of the newspapers. I'll comb through the back issues. Not *Le Figaro*, it's too proper and conservative. But the tabloid types. That stuff's got to be on microfiche now, just like in the States. I'll try to find one of those books in English—you know, those music encyclopedias—*Who's Who in American Music*, or something like that—and see if Haskins's bio is there, and maybe his real name: Ezra Something, or Something Ezekiel—or whatever.

"What I need you to do is try to find back issues of the most obscure kind of music magazines you can think of. Canvass all your street player buddies and ask them if they own such things, or where to start looking. Maybe one of those music journals did a memorial piece on Haskins. Hell, maybe something a little more mainstream—like an early issue of *Rolling Stone*. Those shouldn't be too hard to find. Anything you can think of, no matter how nutty it seems. It's worth a try."

*   *   *

Try we did. None of the arcane, or nutty, sources panned out. But, as I had speculated, there was mention of Little Rube Haskins's death in the police blotter sections of the conventional press. The only report of any length turned up as an ordinary news item in a Paris paper that had long ago ceased publishing. Minimal information emerged on Haskins's career and background—not even where he was born. He was referred to as a black American folk singer who lived at a modest hotel in the 11th arrondissement. In the last report on file (the story had run for two days) Inspector Pascal Simard declared that police were still looking for the vicious killer who had left Monsieur Haskins's mangled body in the one-way street where he resided.

I kind of enjoyed playing the puppet master, dispatching Andre to do this or that spadework. While he was following up one potential lead, I gigged on the street all by myself, which was kind of scary but thrilling. But then the rest of my afternoon was shot, as I had to go hunting for pantyhose long enough for my endless legs. I finally found my size at a little lingerie store where only nuns shopped.

Controlling my other operative, Gigi Lacroix, was a tad trickier. It was tough getting an appointment with him before sundown. He kept hours similar to my friend Aubrey's—the vampire schedule. Daylight must have been rough on his sensitive skin. He finally agreed to meet me at what he daintily referred to as tea time.

Gigi was waiting for me at a sedate "lady food" sort of café near the Louvre. The place was one of those unfortunate pissy hybrids of French and British culture where the waitress sneers at you if your shoes weren't made in

Belgium. No trouble spotting Gigi among all the newly coifed girlfriends in that joint. But at least, thank the baby Jesus, the lovely Martine was not in attendance.

"I have a little news for you," he said, using his napkin to wipe a spray of powdered sugar from his mustache. "Don't get your hopes up too high though."

"What is it?"

"A friend who works the Eiffel Tower says he thinks he knows Tante Vivian."

"What!"

"Yes."

"What do you mean he works the Eiffel Tower? What kind of work?"

"He's a pickpocket. I'm going to see him tomorrow. Chances are he's full of shit and just looking to make a few francs for nothing. But I'll give you a report."

"You won't have to. I'm coming with you."

"No, no, my friend."

"Yes, yes, my friend."

"I said no!" he snarled, without a trace of his usual rueful charm. "It's no fucking place for you, where I'm meeting him. You'll only be in the way. Besides, you'll attract attention to yourself—and me. The last thing I need."

"Well, what about what I need, buster? What the hell kind of place is this where you're meeting?"

"No more questions. You're better off just letting me do what you asked me to do. Anything could happen—*entendu*? You're a Yank, remember. No matter how fancy your French accent is. How would you like to end up deported? Who'll rescue your sweet old aunt then?"

"Why do you put it like that—my 'sweet old aunt'? What are you trying to say, Gigi?"

His laugh was almost as nasty as one of Martine's. "I'm not so sure. But my friend says if this aunt of yours is the same woman he's thinking of, she's up to her old tricks again."

"What the hell does that mean?"

"Hey! Don't break my balls, *'pute*. Those are not my words. They're his. Like I said, he may just be giving me the runaround, anyway. I'll call you. Here . . . try one of these." He proffered his plate, which was crowded with cream-filled delicacies. "A girl with an ass like yours doesn't have to watch her weight. Am I right, *petite*?"

"Gigi," I said in exasperation, "get the fuck back into your coffin."

CHAPTER 8

Mountain Greenery

There it was. Etched in stone: LE PALAIS DU JUSTICE. The palace of justice, eh? I'd be the judge of that.

Actually, police headquarters, which is where I was headed, is next door to the *palais du justice*. The lettering on the police building didn't say a damn thing about justice.

If I'm not mistaken, a number of famous French people—real and fictional—have been associated with the Quai des Orfèvres. The quai was where Inspector Maigret was based, of course. At the urging of my high school French teacher I had read all those George Simenon novels about the eccentric detective. And quite near police headquarters, someone had told me, Simone Signoret and Yves Montand had for years maintained an apartment, in the place Dauphine.

Gigi's news had set me off; although he'd told me to keep cool, that his friend's information might turn out to be bullshit, I couldn't just sit and wait. The more I thought about it the more agitated I became.

Yes, I was standing on the sidewalk looking up at the rather forbidding grandeur of the huge building, the uniformed *flics* buzzing and circling in their evil-looking capes like so many gossiping wasps. But no, I had not decided to throw in the towel and seek police help in finding Vivian. Not yet—not exactly.

I presented my valid passport and an old NYU identification, and I told the liaison officer my story: how I was an American law student doing a paper on police procedure in New York as compared to Paris. I would not presume to take up the time of any of the hardworking detectives on the force today, but I was wondering if he could put me in touch with an Inspector Pascal Simard, whose name I had come across in some old newspaper reportage. Surely the inspector was getting on in years now? and mightn't he have a little time on his hands these days?

Just enough of the truth, mixed with a few Nanette-type whoppers, to be believable. Or so I hoped. My reluctance to involve the authorities stemmed in part from the fear they'd discover Vivian was doing something not on the up-and-up, and the last thing I wanted to do was bring any heat down on her. On the other hand, if they embarked on some kind of investigation of *me*—so what? I had my passport, airline ticket, and ample spending money. I was staying with a nice young man in a borrowed apartment in a nice part of town and we had done nothing wrong.

The French had invented bureaucracy. Were they proud of it, or embarrassed? I didn't know. But at least their red tape appeared to work, sometimes with remarkable efficiency. After the requisite number of phone calls and hours spent waiting in this queue or that anteroom—and the inevitable break for lunch—I was told that Inspector Simard, who had retired to his home in the Loire Valley, had agreed to speak to me. I was given his address and phone number in a town near Amboise, some two hundred kilometers southwest of Paris.

Andre had never actually been outside the city limits and I was letting him know how unParisian I thought that was. After all, you have to spend time in the provinces before you decide you hate them, right? So, wary as he was of my latest plan, he agreed to make the trip with me. First of all, Andre put no faith in anything Gigi or Martine said. He didn't believe I'd ever get that "report" on the Eiffel Tower pickpocket's tip. And second, he probably would have insisted on going with me to Simard's place anyway, to prevent me from doing anything *too* dumb. We had not been together very long, but already he had taken on the role of fool catcher: grabbing me by the shirttails and pulling me back to safety whenever my enthusiasm had me stepping off into the abyss.

We caught an early morning train at the Gare d'Austerlitz and in about two hours we were in Amboise. A local bus took us to the edge of Inspector Simard's village. We made a call to him from the *tabac*, and from there, following the good inspector's directions to the letter, we walked the velvet-plush paths until we arrived at his home.

Monsieur Simard had a full head of silky white hair under the panama hat he tipped to us when we found him in his garden. He must have been in his early seventies but there was no suggestion of a stoop in his bearing. He was as tall and upright as Andre.

Before inviting us inside he turned to me with a questioning look on his face. "I wonder if you know any gardening secrets, mademoiselle."

"Me? Less than nothing."

"Pity," he said. "I have the feeling these flowers need more water. But then again one doesn't want to risk drowning them, you know. I've always liked the garden so much, but it was really my wife who tended to it. I've been slowly killing off one of her prized bushes after another ever since she died ten years ago."

As he invited us inside I thought I saw a mischievous little smile at the corner of Inspector Simard's mouth, but I couldn't be sure. So I just nodded my head in sympathetic understanding.

In less than twenty minutes I had come clean with the inspector. Simard, retired or not, had not lost his touch for eliciting confessions. I told him first about our interest in the Rube Haskins case, and this led inevitably to the saga of Aunt Vivian and my reluctance to involve the authorities. The only thing I left out was the Gigi Lacroix angle. It might be okay for me to make a clean breast of things, but I knew I had no business implicating anybody who'd been in trouble with the law.

After listening attentively to my tale, in a confession of his own he admitted, "The Haskins case is one that still occupies my mind. Even to this day."

"Because you never caught the murderer, you mean," said Andre.

"Yes, of course," answered Simard. "Of course because of that. But I also thought every other element of the case was, well, strange, for lack of a better word. The newspapers—and many of my colleagues, alas—either ignored this poor man's tragic death or dismissed it as a seamy sort of thing—as though Monsieur Haskins had probably lived the violent, dissipated life as a barroom performer and could expect no more than to die terribly."

"Just how terribly did he die?" I asked. "I remember one article referring to a 'mangled' body."

"Oh, believe me, it was a vicious murder. The hatred behind it—the passion, if you will—was quite apparent. But as for your acquaintance—the old gentleman who told you that Monsieur Haskins was involved in a drunken brawl—I'm afraid he has the story all wrong.

"Monsieur Haskins, who probably *was* a bit drunk at the time of his death, was cornered late at night in a little cul-de-sac and struck with a car. But that was not enough for the killer. He or she ran over the body repeatedly, deliberately. It made for a revolting sight."

The inspector sniffed at the air a bit and then lit a cigarette.

My God, I found myself thinking, are you French! I was captivated by the old man. Andre was, too, apparently. He couldn't seem to take his eyes off the inspector. I wondered fleetingly whether Andre would grow into a version of this kind of elderly gentleman—part De Gaulle, part Jackson (Milt, that is, the one from the MJQ).

"No," Inspector Simard continued, "there was no evidence that Monsieur Haskins had seduced anyone's wife or been involved in anything the least bit scandalous. He had no enemies as far as I could determine. He seemed to have been a decent man who was serious about his music and happy to be able to make a living out of it. Happy to have found a home in Paris, where he had a decidedly small but loyal following. The whole thing was not only a mystery but a pity. I've always liked and respected artists, you know."

"Don't tell me," Andre said, incredulous, "that you were a fan of Little Rube's."

"No," the inspector said, "I never heard of the man until he showed up as a file on my desk. I don't know a great deal about the American blues genre. Though I quite enjoyed the jazz I heard in New York years ago, when I was posted for a year with an anti-terrorist mission to the United Nations. I particularly enjoyed hearing Monsieur Getz at the Café Au Go Go. Tell me, is it still there?"

Andre and I exchanged amused glances. The pileup of musical coincidences was getting surreal: just last night we had discovered a cache of old vinyl in the apartment and we'd listened to Getz recorded live at the Au Go Go in 1964.

I related the story to the old gentleman, adding "Sometimes, the world seems a little too small for comfort, Inspector Simard. If you know what I mean."

French shrug. "But of course."

"Let me ask you this," I said to the inspector. "As I told you, we're sure that Haskins was the man whose picture we found in my aunt's book. Only she called him Ez."

"Yes."

"All right. Number two: Haskins was born in America. This thing about his being an escapee from a chain gang in the South may be true or may be mythological. But suppose—whatever he did or was back in the States—

suppose the person who killed him was somebody from his past in America. Could be that he tracked him here. Could have been someone who had no idea Haskins was here, but he finds himself in Paris on business or vacation. And then he discovers that his old enemy Rube is living in Paris and singing at a local club. Whatever wrong Haskins did to this person is still fresh in his mind. So he rents a car—or steals a car—or hires someone—whatever—and kills Rube Haskins and then goes sightseeing and washes his hands of it. You never find the car that was used to commit the murder. The guy gets away scot free."

Simard smiled upon me. "All true, mademoiselle. Sound thinking."

Andre gave my hand a quick, strong squeeze.

"At the time, my thoughts turned in pretty much the same direction," Simard went on. "But there was a limit to how much could be done about all that. Monsieur Haskins held a Canadian passport, and the authorities there said he had no criminal record and no living relatives. Perhaps he obtained the passport with false documents—who knows? My inquiries to the United States never turned up any record of a Rube or Rubin Haskins as an escaped prisoner. But then, I never knew about this possible alias of his—Ez. And of course it was impossible to check on the whereabouts and background of every American tourist in town at the time of Monsieur Haskins's death. It was highly frustrating, you see. All those dead ends."

"And you have no memory of a woman's name coming up in your inquiries—Vivian Whatever?"

"I don't think so, no."

"Seems like this decent, humble little sharecropping poet covered his tracks very well," I commented sourly.

"I agree," said Simard. "And perhaps that helped to guarantee that we would never find his killer. A mystery and a pity, *n'est-ce pas?*"

"Hmm. Listen, speaking of small worlds," I said, "I don't suppose you have an attractive older black woman working in the bakery up the road who might be my aunt Vivian, do you?"

I got my laugh out of him. Then he insisted that we stay and share the lunchtime meal he was preparing.

The inspector asked me to pick a few flowers for the table. While I was doing so, I watched Andre as he played with Monsieur Simard's two old dogs. Yep, I could see my nearsighted love—who wanted so badly to be a Frenchman—in his gray dreadlocks, a retired professor, walking slowly through the village, lost in his thoughts, a few of the town children greeting him as he passed. Sitting by the fire and flipping through the books and recordings that had made him famous. Playing his violin for relaxation before he turned in. *But where am I?* Where am I in that silly daydream? Am I ten years dead, like Madame Simard? Did I die tragically in an automobile accident? Or did I simply leave him—or he me—in Paris, while we were still young?

Lunch turned out to be a near-inedible salad made with greens from his vegetable garden. The bread, however, was very good.

CHAPTER 9

Parisian Thoroughfare

"Oh, what a head I have today, children!"

Morris Melon was drinking a fizzy concoction from the stainless steel tumbler of the bar blender.

The old wag-scholar-expatriate was looking ragged, his big bean-shaped head lolling around on his neck.

We all took our places at the long table where the Bricktop staff ate their supper before the doors opened for the dinner crowd.

The potatoes were superb and the steak with onions was fork tender. The collards had an indefinable Parisian spin—piquant but not too spicy. And oh those hot rolls! Taking second or possibly third helpings from the circulating platters, Andre was boarding, as my grandmother used to say of anyone going at his food with gusto.

I got up and refilled the ice pack that Morris Melon had been pressing to the back of his neck.

"Thank you, young girlfriend." He moaned and buried

his face momentarily in the cold. "Oh . . . Oh, Father, that's better."

The meal proceeded—waiters gossiping and grousing, pitchers of lemonade and tea and wine crisscrossing and changing hands. It was the idealized image of restaurant worker camaraderie. A family *you* choose, rather than the other way around. The kind of thing you see as a lonely teenage nerd and fasten on. It takes actually getting a job as a waitress and standing on your feet seven or eight hours at a time—not to mention the asshole customer factor—to disabuse you of your romantic notions about restaurant work. I lasted about six minutes one summer, trying to make some bucks for the next semester at school.

Old Melon, about halfway back to the land of the living, retired to his office to nap, sipping from a glass of tomato juice as he shuffled off.

Gigi Lacroix showed good timing. Andre and I had just finished our set and repaired to the bar when I was called to the telephone. The pickpocket was not just pulling his chain, after all, he said. Gigi was in Les Halles now, and we should come to meet him in the square across from the Centre Pompidou. Martine would join us for a drink.

Oh goody. The four of us back together again. I knew Andre would be overjoyed to hear it.

I snatched my man's wineglass out of his hand and began tugging at him. "Let's go."

He grumbled and fussed the whole ride on the métro. Not only were we going to be rooked out of more money by the fatuous Gigi, he pointed out; we were heading into the nighttime carnival that is Les Halles, which was always pumping with ugly tourists and junkies and panhandlers and runaways and the dreaded wandering mimes in their cheap French sailor shirts and ghostly white makeup.

"Just where I feel like going at the end of a long day," he spat at me.

I rolled my eyes and endured it. I could endure just about anything. We were closing in on Viv!

It took ten or fifteen minutes to locate Gigi. Lady Martine was the first pointer. I saw her moving toward us, more swiftly than I ever thought possible, considering the height of her heels. I damn near mistook her for one of those mimes; that's how white her face was. And her red mouth was hanging open in dumb amazement. In fact, even the wetness at the corner of her eye seemed to be frozen there, as if painted on—a comic teardrop.

I put out a hand to stop her, but she brushed right past me, moving even faster. When we began to follow, calling out her name, she became a human rocket. The night swallowed her up.

Andre and I walked back in the direction we'd started out. Gigi sat waiting for us not ten yards away.

A hapless young girl with an ice cream cone, who was about to sit down and rest on the same bench Gigi was occupying, must have seen what we saw at about the same moment. Propped up against the armrest, Gigi was leaking blood from the gaping wound in his side. And those flirty, lying eyes of his: dead, dead, dead.

I caught the glint of a big thick blade on the ground.

I dug my nails into Andre's flesh so deep he nearly buckled. But we kept silent and kept right on walking.

Plop! went that ice cream. Lord, could that girl scream.

CHAPTER 10

What Is There to Say?

*N*o, no, no! No you're *not*! You're *not* going! That's only your panic talking!"

It seemed to me that he was the one who was panicking. His voice was up in the ether and his body was shaking.

"Damn right, it's panic talking," I said. "Wouldn't you say it's about time to panic? Somebody just offed Gigi."

Andre swallowed, hard, and rushed over to the refrigerator. He upended the bottle of Vittel water and didn't stop drinking until it was empty.

"I'll tell you what you oughta be doing, my brother," I said tartly. "You ought to be packing your own stuff and leaving with me."

"That is not an option, Nanette." His voice had suddenly taken on that kind of deepness you might hear in an opera, when the baritone is letting somebody know he means business. "End of discussion."

"Well, okay, fuck you, end of discussion."

"Okay, okay, let's try to look at things a little more calmly here, Nanette. Let's make some tea or something and talk about this."

"I don't want any fucking tea!" I screamed.

He slammed the kettle into the wall and bellowed, "Then let's not fucking have any!"

That settled me down.

He began speaking very slowly, focused, oddly menacing. "What I'm trying to get at here, Nan, is this: something very bad has happened, yes. Gigi is dead, yes. But you didn't do it, and you didn't cause it. You're guilty of nothing—understand? Therefore, you have no reason to run. You have no reason to leave me."

"I'm leaving Paris, Andre, I'm not leaving *you*."

"Would you like to explain to me how you can do one without doing the other?"

"Okay, the way I put that was dumb. But you know what I meant. Look, I took on this insane project, to find my aunt, under totally false pretenses. I was bullshitting my mother and bullshitting myself—I admit that now. I thought I could use my Paris smarts to find her. That we'd have a fabulous reunion and I'd give her her money and I'd eat like a king and party like mad and go home happy. Slick little Nan, living by her so-called wits, puts another one over on the grown-ups and lives to tell the tale. I was supposed to rescue her, get it? I never dreamed things were going to turn out like this—so weird—so horrible.

"I'm in over my head now, sweetheart. Don't you understand? The old Nanette karma has kicked in again. Even when I set out with the best intentions in the world, somebody always ends up with a safe falling on their head. I'm the world's biggest authority on turning sugar to shit. It's such a curse that it's almost like a talent."

I saw him trying to get in a word, but I wouldn't let him. "No, no, it's true, Andre. If I hadn't hired that oily little guy he'd be alive today."

"There's no way on earth for you to know that," he protested, trying mightily to keep his tone even. "Gigi was a petty criminal. Maybe even not so petty. That's how he made his living. Who did he associate with: pimps, whores, pickpockets. His death could have had nothing to do with you—I mean us. Hell, maybe it didn't even have anything to do with him. I mean, look where he was hanging out. He could've just been mugged and tried to fight back. Being in the wrong place at the wrong time—that's how it is in every city in the world."

"Oh, come on, Andre. Do you really believe that?"

"I don't know what to believe, Nan. I don't know what happened to him any more than you do. I just know we didn't kill him. Maybe that bitch of his did it."

"Martine did not kill that man," I proclaimed. "You saw her. You saw what she looked like. She came upon him the same way we did. And ran. The same way we did."

"All right, so she didn't do it. So she ran away. What do you think she's going to do now, accuse you? No. She wanted to get as far away from the scene as she could. People like Martine and Gigi don't go to the police. The police come to them."

"That's right! That's my point. And what's going to happen when they find her? She'll tell them about Viv. 'People like Martine' don't just grit their teeth and go off to jail. They start bargaining with the cops. They rat on their cohorts. Vivian and you and I will be implicated."

"Listen to yourself! We're not her motherfucking cohorts, Nan. And why should Martine end up in jail if she didn't kill the guy?"

"Why, why, why? Stop asking me that!" I shouted in frustration. "Why are you being so dense? Why do you refuse to see the connections between Vivian and all the crazy shit that's happened?"

"Because if there is a connection, it isn't crazy. There's a reason for it. And because I don't believe in karma. I don't believe in voodoo. I don't believe in curses. You're not a curse, Nan."

I started laughing grimly. "I'm what? A blessing?"

"Yeah. Or something like that. What else do you call it, what's happened between us?"

"Listen, Andre. I'm never going to be able to sort this out if we don't keep things separate."

"Separate?"

"Yes. Vivian. Missing. In trouble. And somehow—we don't know how, but somehow—mixed up in Gigi's killing. Rube Haskins a.k.a. Ez Whatever the fuck his name was. Martine. *All* that shit on one side. And on the other side, you . . . and me."

"I'm not keeping anything separate, Nan. I've had it with being separate. The last person who 'separated' from me left me with a lousy insurance policy and my dad's Al Green records."

"Please—*please*—" I jerked away from his embrace. "Let me think!"

"Think of what, more reasons to leave?" He grabbed me again and once again I twisted out of his grip.

He stepped off from me then and removed his spectacles. I stood there in silence watching him as he polished them deliberately, compulsively, finally abandoning them on the table.

"What if I can find her?" he said at last.

"Find who?"

"Vivian. What if I find her for you? Will you stay then?"

"How are you going to do that, Andre? We've been jumping through hoops trying to find her."

"Not the right ones, obviously. We didn't do it right."

"I don't want you going to the police, Andre. Don't do it. Do you hear me?"

"What if I find Martine? What if I make her talk—tell me who this pickpocket was who saw Vivian?"

I tried to answer him, but he wouldn't let me. "What if I figure out who killed Rube Haskins? What if I can get the answers to these things—even just one of them—would it be enough to make you stay? Say yes and I'll leave right now and I will find something for you. Will you give me just one more day and let me try?"

"Jesus Christ, Andre, it's two in the morning."

"Will you?"

"But—"

"Will . . . you . . . do it?"

"Yes, yes!" I shouted. "All right."

"All right," he echoed. "Just don't pull away from me again. Just don't, Nan." He gathered me to him, nearly crushing me.

"Andre, don't do it. What if something goes wrong?" I said. "If something happens to you, what'll I do, baby? I'll go crazy."

"Nothing's going to go wrong. Just stay here. Just wait. No plane reservations, no packing, no leaving. Wait here for me. Okay?"

I nodded yes. "Andre?"

"What?"

"Don't forget your glasses."

"Girl, now I *know* you out of your mind!"

"I know, I know," I said wearily. "Please, Aubrey, don't bust my chops over this anymore. I'm kind of at the end of my rope here. Wait. Hold on a minute. I'm getting a cigarette."

I pulled the pack of filtered Gauloises and a packet of matches from the kitchen counter and ran back to the telephone.

I hadn't even bothered to calculate what time it was in New York. Perhaps I had awakened her in the middle of the night. She didn't sound sleepy, though, and I didn't really care. I just knew I had to talk to her.

Just as Inspector Simard had done, she asked few questions, merely listened while I recapped my activities over here and my efforts to locate Vivian:

Taking a room at the low-rent hotel. Checking all the fleabags in town. Checking the hospitals and the morgue. First the dueling banjos bit with Andre down in the métro, then making friends with him. The feeling that someone had been in my room. Searching Vivian's suitcase and finding the Ez photograph and the hundred dollar bill. Placing the ad in the *Trib*. The move to Andre's place and our playing on the street and at Bricktop's. Taking on Gigi Lacroix as a consultant. Martine's rap about the genius of Rube Haskins. The tip Gigi received about

Viv. The Rube Haskins/Ez mystery. The visit to Simard. The discovery of Gigi's corpse. And finally, Andre running out into the night.

"Nanette, if I didn't know you for all these years, I wouldn't believe a word of this story," Aubrey said. "But 'cause I do, I know it's all true. Fact, you probably haven't even told me the worst of it yet. Goddammit. Other people just don't have your fucking life, girl."

Her voice had taken on that edge of maternal outrage that I both resented and craved. With Mom, I had always been so fundamentally secretive about my life that she didn't have a lot to bust my chops over. Aubrey, on the other hand, had plenty of ammunition. She not only knew in excruciating detail about all the messes I got myself into, she usually played a role in getting me out of them. Where I was a dedicated spendthrift, she was shrewd with her money. Where I tumbled time after time after time into these ensnarling, take-no-prisoners affairs with men, she was cool and guarded with her feelings, could play a man like a tin whistle, and was always the one to walk away first. My childhood friend Aubrey Davis, tough bitch that she was, was unfailingly there when I required a killer pair of high heels for the evening, a sympathetic ear for my man troubles, or simple forgiveness. In short, she had earned the motherly stance—outrage and all—she sometimes took toward me.

In a voice thick with intimidation she demanded, "And who is this Jamaican Negro you're living with, Nan?"

"He's *not* Jamaican. I said he had dreads. He's kind of a mulatto from Detroit and his folks are dead and—God, I wish I could tell you—I wish I could tell you everything about him." Yeah, yeah, I knew how sickening this kind of rhapsodizing could get. But I couldn't stop myself. "Like I said, I met him down in the subway. He saved me from these racist geeks. And he's just so young and sensitive and serious and I don't want to hurt him, Aubrey, I can't, I—oh, shit—I guess I love him," I said hopelessly.

She was silent for a minute, gathering her patience, I suppose, trying to calm down, trying not to treat me as the fool she knew me to be.

"What does he look like?" she asked sheepishly.

"Child, he's so gorgeous you could die."

The both of us laughed for a long time.

"I'm not lying, girl. He's got these beautiful bony wrists and fingers and these long arms like a Watusi."

"Like a what?"

"Never mind. Let me tell you about his mouth, Aubrey. At the edges it goes down, but then it goes up again, see, like a surprise. You know what I mean? And you know how some guys have a butt that starts right underneath their waist? His is like that. And his legs are so long, they're almost as pretty as yours. And he has these humongous feet that make me want to cry when I look down at them at night, they're so—so big and awkward and the back of his ankle is so thin you don't know how he can stand up on it."

"Nan!"

"I know, I know, I know."

"You have to pack up and get out of there, girl. You could end up being tapped for that pimp's murder. The police ain't gonna hear about finding your aunt Viv. Or about Andre's butt. What are y'all going to do if they point the finger at him? If the cops over there are like they are over here, they ain't gonna look no further than the first black man they can put their hands on. They'll put his long legs *under* the jail."

That one hadn't occurred to me yet.

Since we found Gigi, I had run a whole world of horrible possibilities through the washing machine of my paranoia. For reasons I couldn't begin to explain, I felt that instead of helping Vivian I was putting more heat on her. I didn't know how, I just knew the danger to her was growing.

But I hadn't thought of the danger to Andre—Andre, who had from the very beginning wanted nothing to do with Gigi. My God, I *was* doing it again: I was calling down death and destruction on those I loved.

"You're right, Aubrey," I said. "I know you're right. I told Andre it was time for me to go. That we had to give up on the Vivian thing. That I had to go home. But he won't hear it. He begged me to give him another day."

"Another day for what? What's he going to find out in a day that y'all couldn't find out in two weeks?"

"Nothing, obviously. I just couldn't bear him nagging me anymore. See, for him it's not about finding Vivian. He wants me to stay here maybe permanently. He wants to—"

"What? What does he want?"

"I don't know. Get married, I think. Or something."

"You kidding."

"He's young, Aubrey."

"How young?"

"He was twenty-seven last month."

"That's only a year and half younger than you are, fool."

I nodded slowly, as if she were there in the room with me.

"Nan?"

"What?"

"You not going to marry that man. I know it's good, girl. But you are not marrying a Geechee street-violin-playing Negro from Detroit. It's stupid, Nan. I don't care how cute he is and I don't care how intelligent he is or what he does to you at night. He got his head up in the same cloud as you, Nanette. He'll never have no money, he can't take care of business, and he can't take care of you. And you belong back here."

I fell silent.

"Nan!"

"Yeah, I'm here."

"Start packing."

I began to cry, hiding it.

"I'm not playing, Nanette. Start packing."

"Right. Will you call Mom like I asked?"

"Yes, girl. Ima call her as soon as you hang up. And you gonna call me when you get a flight out."

CHAPTER 11

What'll I Do?

I fell asleep in my clothes. Everything—shoes, skirt, top, underwear.

I'd felt sorry for myself plenty of times before. I'd been in that valley of indecision and self-pity and regret more times than I cared to recall. It had never felt quite like this before.

It was a restless, heavy kind of sleep. Hideous dreams about everything from being lost in the play yard at age four, to facing my father with a D in my grade book, to my grandmother's ravaging cancer.

I had told Andre on that day I checked out of the hotel: I bonded with another man once in this same way—all at once, and right down to the bone. *It ended up terrible.* Be warned, young man. Black widow Nan will get you.

I heard his key in the door.

To hell with everything else. He was back.

He had been unable to find Martine, let alone Aunt Vivian. Unable to come up with anything new. I knew that he wouldn't. You have to let yourself hope. But I knew he wouldn't. Still, he was safely back home. He looked like shit.

We cried in each other's arms. I don't even know if we knew why we were crying. And perhaps we weren't crying for the same reasons. In any case the tear fest seemed to both exhaust and reanimate us. At the end of it, he reached into his back pocket, extracted a palm-sized object of plastic, and tossed it on the table.

"What is that?" I asked.

"The total fruits of my labors," said Andre. "I asked a couple of the musicians I've met playing on the street to help me find Martine last night. We never did. But one of them found this in his girlfriend's apartment. It's a bootleg Rube Haskins tape. She bought it at a flea market."

That sent us not into tears but hysterical laughter. Laughter that threatened to revert back to tears.

"Play it, Andre. I want to know what kind of chops this son of the South had."

He shook his head. "In a while," he said, sounding like an old man. "Let's go to bed now. You get undressed."

Well, *quel* morning.

We made love until noon—dozing, waking, doing it again, falling off again, waking each other from bad dreams, kissing, promising, doing it again. Finally, he fell asleep still inside me.

The late afternoon bustle down in the street woke us. I'd never been so hungry in my life. I put on the coffee and Andre jumped into some clothes and went out to the market for food.

I bathed, set the table, changed the sheets, tidied the apartment, watered the plants, made a pot of coffee, drank it, and made another.

He'd been away for ninety minutes by then.

By the time another hour went by, I knew.

CHAPTER 12

Poor Butterfly

I forgot to comb my hair, I thought, absurdly.

I bet I look like Martine, I thought. Eyes like pinwheels. Breathing through my mouth and probably drooling.

Help me! I was screaming inside my skull. *Somebody help me!*

But of course I made no sound as I ran through the neighborhood. I was hoping for a miracle. Hoping I'd see him sitting in the café. Hoping he was waiting on line for a pound of ham at the open market. Hoping he had run into one of his musician acquaintances or was shooting the breeze with the guy in the wine store. Hoping, even, that he'd been hit by a motorcycle and been taken to the hospital with a nice, safe, lovely broken leg.

I ran blindly down into the métro and back out again.

I went back to the apartment, still running, still hoping, still screaming inside.

No Andre.

I couldn't catch my breath. "What'll I do baby, I'll go crazy," I wailed.

I was talking to myself.

I went on talking: "No—Don't go out again. Stay by the phone. No, use the phone. Call! Call somebody."

Inspector Simard didn't answer. Where the hell was he? In that stupid garden of his? Drinking wine out on the lawn as the sun went down? Having coffee with the postman in the town bar? I pictured his two lazy brown dogs looking up in boredom at the ringing telephone.

I went rummaging in the liquor cabinet, knocking over a couple of those goddamn useless little cordial glasses. All I could find was a bottle of Jamaican rum. I poured out a huge glass and gulped it. No cigarettes in the house. I pulled at my hair until my scalp ached.

Simard answered on the second try.

"Ah! *Salut,* mademoiselle. Are you well? I was thinking of you and your friend only last—"

I stopped him there and began to babble out the story in that kind of fractured French for which the Academie Française would have brought back the death penalty.

Gigi Lacroix no longer needed my discretion, my protection from the authorities. I told Simard what I'd omitted from my story before.

"That was not a very wise course to follow," he commented softly at the end of the tale.

A masterpiece of understatement.

And then he added, "It might have been better for you to have disclosed this to me during your visit."

I sighed into the receiver, not out of exasperation but grief. The sigh soon became a sob. I cried my heart out while he hung on at the other end, making no sound except to clear his throat periodically.

"Very well, very well then," he said at last. "Listen carefully, young one. The *sûreté* will not undertake a search for Monsieur Andre for at least another forty-eight hours. But you must get the wheels turning a great deal faster than that.

"I will give you the name of a lieutenant at the Quai des Orfèvres. He will contact you later, after I've had a chance to locate and speak to him. But first, go to your embassy. Do it right away. It does not matter what you tell the consul about how your friend came to be missing. The authorities are accustomed to dealing with young people in trouble. Tell them . . . Well, you are obviously adept at inventing things. Or tell them the truth, if it appears warranted. The important thing is that you go to them now. *Entendu?*"

"Yes, sir," I said, sniveling.

"Go now," he said sternly, "but first, some other advice."

"Yes?"

"I know you are a brave, independent young person, and that you are trying to do the honorable thing. But I ask you this, mademoiselle: How good an actress are you? How good are you at being a Frenchwoman?"

"What do you mean?"

"Only this: It will not do to go to the embassy, and especially not to the Paris police, as a hysteric demanding action. Present yourself as a respectable young woman, one who has taken a misstep perhaps—but a *woman,* if you take my meaning. *Une femme française.* Cry discreetly, cross your legs demurely, show how distraught you are over the disappearance of the man you love. But do not become shrill in the face of their lassitude."

Got it. The basic damsel-in-distress riff. Get the men to do what you want. Could I pull it off? Here was yet another occasion for me to wish that I was Aubrey.

On the other hand, if I wasn't genuinely in distress right now, then what in God's name could distress possibly mean?

While Simard instructed me, I began undoing my jeans and searching the room frantically with my eyes. Where were my pantyhose?

"Inspector?" I said.

"*Oui?*"

"Do you think he's still alive? Do you think that's possible?"

He didn't hesitate at all. "Of course I do. You love him, *n'est-ce pas?*"

I knew fully how little logic there was in his enigmatic answer. Still, it made sense to me, and I had to hang on to it. I rang off.

But before I could take my femme act on the road, it became academic.

As I was wrestling horribly with the back zipper of my dress, the telephone rang. I pounced on it, thinking, Thank you, God/Allah/Siva/Sojourner Truth. I'd rather take my chances with Simard's contact at the police department than face an unknown quantity like a white American diplomat—one who, for all I knew, might even turn out to be a woman.

"*Oui, allo!*" I called into the phone.

"Nan."

It was Andre.

I fell to the floor, receiver still in my hand.

"Nan?"

"It's me, sweetheart," I said, matching the grave hush in his voice. I willed my heart to stop pounding so loud. "Something's wrong, isn't it?"

"Yes."

"Are you okay, Andre? I mean, not hurt."

"Yes."

"And someone's there, right? Listening. Telling you what to say."

"Yes."

"What do they want?"

"I told—" He broke off with a sharp intake of breath.

"Andre!"

"It's all right. Just listen. You know how you told me once there used to be a rape crisis center where a friend of yours was a counselor? You remember where that was?"

"Yes, I remember."

"Don't say the name of the street," he cautioned. "Just come there. Now."

"All right. I'm coming."

"Wait a minute! Come alone, right?"

"Yes."

"And bring those papers from home—from New York, I mean. You know what papers I mean, don't you? Bring all of it. You have to bring all of it and you have to come alone, then we'll both be all right. I promise. It's not a setup, understand?"

"Okay," I said, understanding perfectly what he meant by "papers": the money I'd been sent over here to deliver.

The money orders. Someone knew about my mission and was holding Andre until I turned over the money.

Of course, I thought, it had to be the Gigi/Martine underworld connection. I had been stupid enough to go to a petty crook for help, and now I was reaping the wages of that error.

Except I had not been stupid enough to tell them the reason I was looking for Vivian was to turn over an inheritance to her. I'd never said a word to Gigi or Martine or anyone but Inspector Simard about the ten thousand. Yet, somehow, they'd found out.

I was betting Gigi had been killed because of that money.

"Understand everything now?" Andre asked.

The answer to that one, obviously, was no. But that isn't what I said.

"Yes," is what I said, "I'm on the way." I started to ask once more if he was okay, but I realized I was speaking into dead air.

The street he would not let me name was a little cul-de-sac in the 11th, off the rue Chanzy. There is such a thing as the beaten path. There's off the beaten path. And then there is Cité Prost—that's the street Andre was talking about.

I had indeed once known someone who volunteered her time at a women's counseling center there. Andre and I had dropped another musician off in a cab one night and I had pointed the old building out to him.

"Kind of an isolated part of town for something like that, isn't it?" he had asked.

"If you think it's weird now, you should have seen it then," I countered. "When you went in for counseling, you were always looking over your shoulder to make sure somebody wasn't going to rape you."

There was still a slice of sunlight left when I emerged from the métro. The rosy horizon lit my way as I trotted along the avenue, looking for the sharp turn into Cité Prost.

I found it, made the turn, and then halted in my tracks. The grimy street hulked before me like a living presence, a fearsome thing with hollow eyes and wings.

Half the buildings on the street had been razed. Half of those remaining were in some stage of gentrifying refurbishment. Piled building bricks, wheelbarrows, and construction machinery cluttered the sidewalks.

The women's center was all boarded up. I stood on the pavement and waited, staring at the building. Was I expected to go *in* there? My heart froze in my chest. How was I going to get in? I looked around for the inevitable smelly *type* who would emerge from the shadows and take me around the back way. Who else would be inside? Homesteading junkies fixing by candlelight? Lady Martine in her stilettos, the ring leader of some murderous band of outsiders?

Where did they have Andre? The thought of him gagged and locked in a closet or in a corner with his wrists and ankles bound made me tremble. And though I tried willing myself not to think of the worst—that they had killed him as soon as he hung up, as soon as I'd agreed to bring the money—I was losing the battle.

What if they were watching me right now? Killing him right now?

The press of all those gruesome possibilities was too

much. I began to rush toward the building. But a word spoken softly and carried on the mild air stopped me.

"Nan."

I whirled.

Not another soul on the street. I looked around frantically. Up at the bricked-in windows. Even to the branches of a yellowing plane tree. Where had that voice come from?

There was an old gray Volkswagen parked directly across from the center. I hadn't even noticed it before. I walked toward it, slowly. And then I began to cry, making no noise, just weeping silently, happy, grateful: that was Andre sitting behind the wheel. He lifted one hand slightly and beckoned me to him.

I ran to the driver's side and tried to open the door.

"Take it easy, Nan," he said tonelessly. "Go around to the other side and get in."

For a moment I couldn't move to obey him. I was too busy searching his face for bruises, checking his clothing for bloodstains. But then I saw him wince, and he repeated sharply, "Go around and get in, Nan."

I did it on the double.

"Don't turn around yet!" he barked when I had closed the door after me.

It soon became plain what his wincing was all about. There was a gun less than half an inch from the nape of his neck.

"I'm *okay,* Nan, just you be cool," he said desperately, seeing me seeing the black muzzle.

A "titter" came from the backseat then, no other word for it, really. Yeah, a titter—and the motherfucker was girlish as all get-out. Tinkling and merry, and perhaps tinged with madness.

"Yeah, he's *okay*," said the laugher. "And you know what, girl? I want to thank you for letting me borrow this pretty man of yours for the day. We had a lot of fun."

Andre's warnings be damned. I turned around and took a good look. A good hard look.

A silence had fallen in the car. It went on and on and on. I was the one to break it.

"Vivian," I said, "I hate you."

CHAPTER 13

You've Changed

I mean, Vivian, I hate what you're doing. Whatever that is."

"I swear to Jesus," she replied, "sometimes I barely know what I'm doing anymore."

"Here's a suggestion," I said acidly. "Get that gun away from Andre's head. Are you out of your mind!"

The thing was withdrawn and Andre let out an endless breath. I took his hand and held it for a long moment before turning back to my sweet old aunt, as Gigi had once called her.

"I'm not sure you heard me, Viv. I just asked you if you were out of your mind."

Vivian sighed heavily, then, as if she'd just had a hit of B_{12}, demanded breezily, "Where's that money, Nanny Lou? Pretty man here tells me my ship's come in. When I found out you were in Paris looking for me, I figured you'd brought some dough from home. But I never dreamed you were going to make me a rich bitch."

It was my turn to laugh gaily. "Just a minute here, Aunt Viv. Let me get something straight first, okay? You think you can frighten my mother half to death with your stupid telegrams, get me all the way over here, and then, like, *hide* from me—terrorize me—kidnap my fucking boyfriend and hold me up at gunpoint. Then you're gonna call me Nanny Lou, right? Like when you used to bounce me on your knee. Do I have all that right, Aunt Viv?"

"I'm something else, huh?" she said soberly.

Vivian leaned forward a bit. There was gray in her hair now and her eyes were dull, the coppery skin over her thin face not so taut anymore. But she was still my wild auntie. Great bones, high forehead, wide and noble nose with that sexy bump between the nostrils. Still a package of nervous energy and sharp angles. My dad's wayward sister. My baby-sitter and role model, whom I adored. Aunt Vivian. Armed kidnapper and holdup woman.

I couldn't take it in. "Why'd you do it? Why?"

"That makes no difference now. I know I scared you shitless and I'm sorry I had to do it this way. But I want that money, Nan. You give me that money and then you and your young man get on a plane and go home, you understand me? Get out of Paris. This has nothing to do with you and you're going to get burned bad if you stay here."

"Nothing to do with us?" Andre at last spoke up. "Lady, notice I'm not asking you if you're crazy. I already know the answer to that. You've been threatening to blow my head off for several hours now, and you can sit there and say it has nothing to do with us?"

She didn't answer him, head turned away.

"God damn!" he exploded. "I ought to come back there and snatch you—"

I managed to shush him with a hand to his face.

"Who was Ez?" I asked her point-blank.

Snap of the head. Her voice broke as she asked, "What?"

"Come on, Viv. You heard me. Who was Ez? The man who also called himself Little Rube Haskins. And what do you know about the way he died?"

"I'm not going to talk to you all about that. I told you, that's nothing to do with you!" She was gripping the back of my seat tightly as she spoke.

"You heard what Andre just said, Vivian. If it didn't have anything to do with us, we wouldn't be sitting here looking down the barrel of a gun. So cut the shit, auntie. I want to know what's going on here. I want some answers! Were you sleeping with that guy Haskins when you lived in Paris all those years ago? Did you set him up to be killed?" It frightened me to ask the next question, but I did it anyway: "Did you run him down yourself?"

Her fingers tightened on the old upholstery.

"Why did you run from your hotel and why did you make yourself so hard to find? Who told you I was looking for you?" I pressed.

No answer, of course. Just an awful grimace and her knuckles going white.

I began to scream out my questions then: "Did you know a pimp named Gigi who was murdered the other day? Don't just sit there like a mummy, Vivian. You owe me some answers! And don't give me any more of that stupid shit about getting burned, okay? We're already burning."

"All right, Nan, that's enough!" She returned my nasty tone at equal volume. "Stop playing the tough guy, because it isn't going to work with me. There are much nastier guys than you after my ass. And they don't just want to make me apologize for not dropping a line every once in a while. They're trying to kill me."

"*Who!?*" Andre shouted before I got the chance to. "Who's trying to kill you? Jesus Christ, woman, why don't you just tell us what this is about?"

Vivian flinched at his tone. And then she almost smiled. "All right. Listen up, the both of you. I'm going to tell you as much as you need to know, and hope it's enough to convince you to get out of town." She turned those now-sad brown eyes on me.

"I had me a lot of men, Nan. A lot of friends and a lot of coke and a lot to drink—but mainly a lot of men. This particular one," she said slowly, "your father used to call a cracker. To his face. He thought that was funny. But then, as you know, my brother never had much of a sense of humor.

"I don't know why, exactly, don't ask me to explain it, but this one I loved. Jerry Brainard was his name. I don't know if you remember him."

"Kind of," I said. "We found his picture in your album."

She nodded. "You're young, baby. Both of you are. You don't know yet what it does to you when somebody you thought loved you, turns around and puts a knife in you. I don't just mean leaving you. I don't mean hitting you, or fucking around on you, or anything like that. I mean when you love them enough to give them your eyes, and then they actually put you in a position where—where you're going to die. They could've saved you. They could've warned you. But it wasn't convenient for them. You just don't know what that kind of betrayal is like."

Oh, don't I now? I wanted to say. *You really should have dropped a line, auntie. I could have told you some story.*

I had to fight myself to keep from interrupting her, to tell her that, young or not, I'd had almost the identical experience with a man I thought I loved. But I couldn't go into that now. I had to hear *her* ghost story now.

"When we were living here in Paris, it was fabulous," Vivian said, coming alive again, for just a second. "I was over here—speaking French, girl! I had this fine man who was crazy about me and a lot of other men in love with me and all the fun in the world and the party never stopped. Just like back at home. Just like everywhere in those days. Your aunt Viv could hang with the best of them and drink most men under the table. I was bad, baby, I was out there."

"I know," I said.

"Well, the day came when the party *did* stop. Jerry screwed me royally. Took everything I had. But hey, those are the breaks, right? Somebody dogs you like that, it's cold, yeah, but you can walk away from that in one piece.

"No, that wasn't the worst of it by a long shot. See, there was this other fella who was crazy about me, too. He loved me, Nan. This Negro loved me in a way I couldn't begin to understand at the time. And I played him. I played him something shameless."

"You mean Ez. Rube Haskins."

"Yeah. Ez. A sweet little guy who was in way over his head and never knew shit from Shinola. I let him think I could have the same kind of feelings for him that he had for me. And I took him for a lot of money—everything he made from singing and all the front money this German company gave him to make this record. All to help Jerry. I'm not proud of it, Nan. I did a lot of stuff I never should have done—things you'd be ashamed to know about me—things that could have landed me in jail if I'd been caught—but I feel the worst about Little Rube.

"Anyway, what goes around comes around, like they say. I fucked over Ez, and Jerry did the same to me. He made off with more than a hundred and fifty thousand. Except—before Jerry left Paris—before he dumped me—Ez was—"

"He was run down by a car. Murdered," I supplied.

"Yes, that's right."

"Jerry killed him?"

She nodded. "Right. That piece of shit killed him. Wasn't enough that I had ripped him off and tore his heart out. Jerry had to kill him, the poor bastard. The cops looked into it, but they had no suspects. I figured it was only a matter of time before they'd hear something about the woman Ez had been keeping company with. They'd learn about me, come after me. What could I do? I felt horrible for the way it all came down. But it wasn't me who did the killing, and I didn't intend to get cracked for it. Sure, I was ashamed of myself, but I wanted to live. I left here on the run and never stopped running."

"Until you got to the next party," Andre said brutally.

Vivian shot him a bullet of a look. But she didn't deny his words. "That was all a long time ago," she continued. "I did what I had to do to survive. A lot of the stuff I did wasn't very nice. Wasn't the kind of news my family would appreciate hearing. But I never forgot Ez, I never forgot Jerry, and I never forgave.

"I'm about played out now, Nan. Look at me. Do I look like I'm still a party girl? You think all the pretty men still want me? Think anybody wants to use my picture to try and sell nylons or a pack of cigarettes? I don't think so.

"But now I see my chance to get even with Jerry Brainard. To even the score—for me and for Ez. A couple of months ago I heard through some people I know that Jerry was living in Paris again. I decided to come over here and see him, see him one more time—and kill him. I've got to kill him, understand, because he's still at it. Even after all this time he's still trying to bury me."

And Daddy had once voiced the fear that "maybe" Vivian was "accepting money from men." I had to laugh at the memory.

My fabulous aunt Vivian. Next time I guess I should be a little more careful about choosing a role model.

I shook my head. "You can't do it, Viv," I said sadly. "You *can't* get even."

"Watch me," she said, then corrected herself: "No, don't watch me. That's what I'm trying to tell you and this boy. Get out of here so you don't have to watch me. So none of it touches you."

Too late for that.

"What did you mean—that thing about burying you?

You mean Brainard knows you're in Paris and coming after him?"

"Yeah, he knows all right. A piece of scum he sent after me almost killed me one night. If I hadn't been carrying a can of Mace, I wouldn't be here talking to you now. I spotted the same guy hanging around my hotel, waiting for a rematch. Oh yeah, Jerry knows I'm here all right.

"Then, a couple of weeks ago he killed a woman. Or had her killed. A white girl who was working for him. And now the son of a bitch is trying to frame me for it. He's been slowly, steadily turning the cops on to me. He left things I had in my suitcase at the hotel near that girl's body—some old scarf of mine. It looks like the candlestick or whatever it was he used to bash in her skull was mine, too. I can't remember half of what I had in that bag. He's playing some kind of game with me, that old Satan. But he's not going to win. I'm going to get him first, and after that—whatever happens, happens. If I make it out of town, fine. If I don't, fine. But I don't want you here. I don't want you to have to deal with the fallout."

I went back to that morning when Andre and I sat on the hotel bed amid the breakfast dishes, reading about Mary Polk's murder in the morning paper. I recalled the cold ripple that had gone up my back.

Thank God, I had thought then, thank God it isn't Viv lying dead in that alley. I had tossed the newspaper aside and never spoke of the story again. But that killing had worried me, even then. Maybe it was something as ethereal as that little square of fabric on the ground, the one that had indeed been Vivian's Scout bandanna. I don't know. But something had made me fear the murder was no out-of-the-blue occurrence, a tragedy unconnected to our lives. I felt somehow that it did have something to do with us—with Vivian and me. And that it was going to come back on us one day.

"Back up a minute," Andre was saying to Vivian, trying to sound soothing. I knew what he was going to ask her, 'cause I had the same question for her on the tip of my tongue. "What kind of work did the white woman do for him?"

Vivian snorted. "Work? You work for Jerry and Jerry works you. He's been into so many different scams and businesses. He moved dirty money for a while. Computer secrets. Drugs. I don't know what that chick was doing for him. It could have been any one of a hundred things."

"What a sterling fellow you gave your heart to, Viv," I commented. "Did you ever help him in any of his businesses when you were with him? Did he work you?"

Her stiff posture and the way she bit off the words she was about to utter gave me my answer.

My role model had done a bit of everything, it seemed. That pickpocket, whoever he was, the one who made the cryptic remark to Gigi about Viv being up to her old tricks? Guess he hadn't lied either. I no longer wanted to know exactly what he meant by the remark. It didn't matter anymore.

What mattered was shutting my aunt down before she blew away this Satan of an ex-husband and spent what was left of her life in prison. Hell, after all my contortions to keep the authorities out of her business, I now realized she would be better off just telling the police that Brainard had killed Rube Haskins. If they reopened the case and could prove that, she'd have her revenge. If the law in France worked the same way it did in the States, there was no statute of limitations on murder. They could, theoretically, nab you a hundred years after the fact.

Inspector Simard would help us, I was certain, advise us. Viv had done an awful thing beating Haskins out of his money, but he was in no position to bring charges against her for that. And most important, she had nothing to do with the murder.

Now, how was I going to get her to see it that way?

I had had a lot of men, too.

I was going to be thirty in another year and a half. I had lived in Europe. Seen a bit of the world. I'd done my share of dumb things, and God knows I play fast and loose with the truth when it suits my purposes. But I tell myself that I still have a fairly good heart; at any rate, whatever there is in my heart, it ain't larceny. I have a salty tongue sometimes, I'm told. But I'm not a cynic, either. Something beautiful, new, intriguing, sexy presents itself to me, my first instinct is to say yes rather than no.

I had always thought Viv had a lot to do with me being that way. That my determination to be *out there,* as she put it, was due to her influence. Now I wasn't so sure. I just knew she was family, she was in deep shit, and I had to help her.

"I want my money, Nan."

"Okay," I said, stalling. "Tell us where Jerry is now. Do you know where to find him?"

"I know—now I do. But I'm not telling you. How stupid do you think I am, Nanette?"

"Honestly, Viv? I don't know how stupid you are. Excuse me for pointing it out, but you're about to embark on one of the stupidest-ass mistakes I've ever heard of in my life. You've had it bad for a long time, it sounds like. But now you've got ten grand, like a gift from God, and all you can think to do is go to prison for murder. Why don't you rat Jerry out to the cops and then go get yourself a room at the Ritz and start living? Fuck this revenge thing."

"I have my own reasons for doing it this way," she said icily. "Hand over that money."

"All right. Just a minute. Just answer one thing more."

"What?"

"Why on earth did you write home to Mom asking for help—telling her you were broke and stranded?"

"Andre asked me the same thing," she said impatiently. "I already told him. I *was* broke. But I didn't write jack to your mother. I don't know what the hell you all are talking about."

"Then it had to be Jerry who sent the card and the telegram," Andre reasoned.

"That's right," I echoed. "He's been setting you up for something for a while now, Vivian. He's just playing with you. He must've known where you were long before you knew where he was. Why don't you face the fact you're not going to win this game with him? He's going to—"

"I'm through talking, Nan. Give me those checks."

"Vivian, you're not going to put that gun on us again. You're not going to take this all the way there— Oh. I guess you are."

"You think I want to, girl? You're making me do it!" she shrieked. "Just give me the money and stop asking questions!"

I did as she asked.

"All right, Andre," she instructed, "leave the keys and get out."

Frantic, he began to splutter: Where was she taking me? Why couldn't he go, too? If she was going to commit murder, that was her business, but how could she do this to me, her own flesh and blood? Why was she taking me down with her?

"Just . . . get . . . the . . . fuck . . . out. Nan's not going anywhere with me. She's getting out, too."

I climbed out wearily and joined Andre on the sidewalk, Vivian's gun trained on his heart.

"The two of you, get over there in the doorway of that old building. And don't move until I drive away."

"One last time, Viv—" I began to beg.

"I told you, Nanette. I'm through talking. Move!"

We backed over to the abandoned women's center.

"Forget it," I heard Andre say as I craned my neck to read the back license plate. "She's covered up the back one. I never got a look at the front."

We heard the engine turn over.

"You're on the way to the guillotine, Viv," I suddenly shouted across to her. "What do you need that money for?"

Her face appeared for a moment in the window on the passenger side. "I need to buy a gun," she shouted back.

Andre and I looked at each other in puzzlement.

"Here, baby!" she called, sounding young and merry again. "Go play with your toys."

A second later we heard the dull clatter of a metal object hitting the pavement. Then the car zoomed off.

I ran over and picked up the weapon, which was, despite its weight, nothing more than a prop—like she'd said, a toy.

The Volkswagen was nowhere in sight. No, it wouldn't

be. I recalled how Viv had this one boyfriend whose car she would borrow sometimes, a cute red convertible. She drove incredibly fast, like a demon. Cut quite a figure behind the wheel with her pretty hair blowing against the wind.

CHAPTER 14

Do Nothing Till You Hear From Me

The *gardien* for the apartment building told us a police detective had come by to see me. He had left his card and asked me to phone him at the station the moment I got back.

I put the card in my pocket and followed Andre up the stairs and into the apartment.

So my big, strong stud—the love of my life—had been held hostage for five hours by an unarmed hundred-and-five-pound middle-aged lady.

I wanted to yell at him. Ridicule him. Slap him silly. Call him a sissy and an idiot.

I also wanted to laugh.

But I didn't do any of that. I was too tired. And too grateful he was alive. And too mad at Vivian.

I borrowed another phrase from the late Gigi Lacroix. "So you thought you were looking up the ass of death, huh?" I asked Andre. "What was going through your mind? Were you praying? Did you curse the day you met me?"

"Praying that her finger didn't slip," he said quietly. "And I cursed all right. But not you. Your aunt—" The words seemed to fail him there. "God, that bitch is crazy."

He collapsed into the nearest chair and I poured him a stiff drink of the rum I had been guzzling a few hours earlier.

"I don't suppose there's anything to smoke in the house," he asked leadenly.

"I ran out of Gauloises last night."

"No, Nan. I mean something to *smoke*. If ever two people in the world deserved to get high, it's us."

I walked away from him and settled in the chair on the other side of the room. "Listen," I said, "I know what you must be thinking."

"What do you mean? Thinking about what?"

"About Vivian. Deciding what to do."

"Do?"

"Yes. I know you've had it. You're just grateful that you've still got a head on your body. All you want to do is wash your hands of Vivian. And I don't blame you, believe me."

"Wash *my* hands! Nan, she just blew us off. Like you told her, she kills that guy and her problems are just beginning. There's no decision for us to make except who to call first—the cops or the men with the white lab coats and the Thorazine. Vivian's not responsible anymore. She has to be stopped."

"I know that!" I said impatiently. "Yes, of course she has to be stopped. But not by the police. I've got to get her out of here and back home where she can get some help."

"Don't you start with that shit again, Nanette. I'm telling you."

"Andre, what do you want me to do? Send a SWAT team after her? Do you want me to call these people and report she's running around with a real gun now?"

"Do *I* want you to? No. I want her in a straitjacket. And I want you to stop fucking around in this mess so we can live the rest of our lives."

"Andre, they'll cut her down without blinking. She's not responsible anymore. You said it yourself. She's nuts."

"I'm not going to argue with you about this, Nan. Call that detective. Or call Simard. Just do it. But you can't go around like the angel of justice, saving the day for everybody—for your mother, for Vivian, for this bastard Jerry, for dead people even. You got your hands full just barely keeping yourself in one piece—and I mean just."

"Well, thank you so much, Andre. I'm an incompetent, right? And an egomaniac along with it."

"I give up." He dismissed me with a gesture of disgust.

"What—I'm supposed to talk to the hand now?"

He turned his back on me and snapped on the stereo with a violent push of the button. I guess he just wanted to tune me out. A minute later I heard what he was tuning in: the whiny twang of a solo guitar. Startled by the deafening volume, I jumped.

Andre was playing the Rube Haskins cassette he had thrown across the room early that morning. That was some twelve or thirteen hours ago. The morning seemed like a lifetime ago.

I went over to the refrigerator and began searching for food I knew damn well we didn't have.

Plunk plunk splunk! Plunk plunk splunk! went the insistent guitar. I heard Little Rube's voice then. A dusty, pain-filled tremolo telling about the blood-drenched beauty of the South, and how writing these songs had been his way of surviving it. There followed some familiar-sounding blues licks, and then his slave's wail. No doubt he was now performing Martine's fave: "The Field Hand's Prayer."

"Turn it down just a little," I said in the middle of a lively walking blues with barbed lyrics about King Cotton.

Andre was making no move to adjust the earsplitting level.

"Hey, man, did you hear what I said?" I asked belligerently. "Turn that down!"

Andre did not heed me and did not answer. Still furious at me, I supposed.

Halfway through the next selection, he ran over to me and grabbed my elbow. "Listen!" he exhorted, eyes blazing.

"No," I said wearily. "No more talking, no more fighting. I can't stand it anymore. Just give me a minute before I sic the dogs on Vivian. I'll call that cop, okay? I'll turn her in. Will that make you happy, Andre?"

"No no no! Not that. *Listen!*"

I did, for another ten minutes. It was just more of the same.

Haskins talking for a few minutes about the horrors of

life on the chain gang, telling a hair-raising anecdote about the circumstances that led him to write one song or another. Then another tune. Some nice fretwork here and there. A good voice but hardly a riveting delivery. It was true that I didn't have a trained ear for the blues or folk music. I thought the world of Muddy Waters and Bessie Smith, Bobby Blue Bland and Charles Brown and quite a few others, but didn't fancy myself as any kind of expert about the bedrock blues. I worshiped the bebop deities and their inheritors, and so to that extent I knew the blues.

To me, Rube Haskins just wasn't that special. He sounded like a competent musician showing off his stuff. But without any defining style.

In addition to that, the background noises—after all, this was an amateur, bootleg tape—were driving me crazy.

I sighed loudly and then began literally to plead with Andre to turn the tape off.

After he complied, he gave out with an eerie cry of triumph. "I knew it!" he shouted. "I knew it!"

"Excuse me?"

"Nan, Little Rube Haskins is Little Rube Nothing."

"Well, that's a little cold, Andre. I don't think he's so bad."

"No, of course he's not. He isn't bad. He's nothing."

"Explain, please, Professor. You've lost me here."

"You must have been asleep that day in class. That day when the music teacher lectured about the various trips the scholars made down south to record indigenous blues artists. It started even before the twenties, and people did it on and off for the next half century. Most of the stuff on this tape has been lifted from the old cylinders those researchers made. Half the famous blues artists who ever existed were first recorded on those field trips. The Library of Congress gathered hundreds of hours of it. There were even some commercial records issued."

"What!"

"Yes, yes. I'm telling you, Rube Haskins did not write that stuff. He stole it—or coopted it—or whatever you want to call it. I recognize some of the protest stuff this guy Gellert recorded in the thirties. Some of the words have been switched around. Some of the dialect has been cleaned up. But that's what this is. Don't you remember? John and Alan Lomax, these two Southerners—father and son—"

"Oh my Lord—yes! And the venerable Zora Neale Hurston took part in it, too," I interrupted. "I'm remembering it now. And for your information, I might have dozed off once in a while in ethnic studies, but I never fell asleep in music class, mister."

Andre was almost drooling by that time. "If I ever have the misfortune of seeing that lowlife bitch Martine again, her ass is mine," he said.

If I was remembering the story right, they would sometimes go into the prisons and record these black men singing their chain gang blues. Unbidden, the image of a rickety jailhouse in the Mississippi sun sprang into my head. What Andre had said about the future blues stars first being recorded as part of an anthropological study might be true. But what about all those anonymous men and women—musicians—nobody had ever heard of before, and never heard of again? Rube Haskins had ripped them off. The sweet country boy who didn't know shit from Shinola knew enough to do that. I found I was oddly disappointed in Little Rube. I must have needed to believe in his purity. I was truly shocked that he was turning out to be as dishonest as Vivian was.

"You know that's how Leadbelly was discovered, don't you?" Andre was saying. "Terry and McGhee, too."

"Right, right," I answered, distracted, fretting.

Andre was giving me the capsule version of the life of Sippie Wallace now. I liked her, too, but I wasn't concentrating. I began to pace furiously while he alternately pontificated and sadistically, scatologically set out what he'd like to do to Martine and every condescending, ignorant black-music manqué like her.

"Andre?"

"Huh?"

"Shut up."

"Huh?"

"I've got to make a call."

"Inspector Simard? It's Nan Hayes."

"*Oui.* What has happened? Did you see my young friend from the prefecture?"

"I'll tell you about that in a minute," I said. "First of all, Andre is safe. He's here, with me."

"I am relieved."

"Yes. Me, too. Now I have to ask you something else. I know it sounds strange, but please just tell me. It's important."

"If I can, young one. What is it?"

"Do you recall, Inspector, when you were working the Rube Haskins case, if there was ever any mention of the name Jerry Brainard?"

There was a long silence. When at last he answered

non, it seemed to be with great hesitation; that one-word answer was heavy with meaning.

"Why did you say it that way, Monsieur Simard? Please tell me. Do you recognize the name or not?"

"Actually, yes, I do."

"You mean he was questioned in the murder investigation?"

"No, never. I know that name for quite a different reason. Brainard was well known to the police. He was suspected of counterfeiting as well as several other crimes, large and small. But we were unable to put him away. He associated with a host of known criminals, but we were never able to catch him at anything. He cut a path between America and Paris, Toulouse, Marseilles for years. But he was uncommonly careful. Tell me why you are asking about this man."

"Because my aunt—because Andre and I know now that he was my aunt's husband. Vivian and Brainard scammed Haskins out of all the money he had. Then Brainard deserted her. And listen to this: he's the one who killed Rube Haskins."

"*Comment?* He did what?"

"It's true, Inspector. And now we've got to do something before he ruins another life—causes another death."

"But how did you . . . Are you certain about this?" Simard asked doubtfully.

"Well, yes. And no. I mean—please tell me, what are you holding back?"

"Mademoiselle Hayes, Brainard escaped punishment for many years. But I don't see how he could cause ruin to anyone at this time, or ever again. He was murdered only last month."

Another one! How many blows to the head was I expected to sustain in one twenty-four-hour period?

"But that can't be," I insisted. "It can't."

I was convinced he had made a mistake. Vivian had just told us she'd been in Paris for a couple of months. If that was true, she had to know Jerry had been murdered. How could she not know? She had distinctly said she knew where Jerry Brainard was right now—that she was going to get him as soon as she obtained a weapon. It meant she was chasing a dead man. Taking her revenge on a dead man.

"Are you sure it was the same Jerry Brainard who was killed?" I asked.

The inspector answered huffily, "I am no longer with the department, but I can still read the newspapers. It was there for anyone to see."

I hung on to the receiver a long time, trying to digest this latest news, my mind racing as it grabbed hold and then let go of one slippery fact after another; as I tried to sort out the sane from the insane; figure out who was crazy and who was merely a liar.

"What's he saying? *What's he saying?*"

I batted Andre away from me.

"Hello—Mademoiselle?" the inspector called.

"Yes, yes," I snapped, rude as could be. "I have to go now."

"*Ne quittez pas, mademoiselle!* Don't hang up yet! Have you seen my friend from the department? If you know anything about this murder, you must tell him."

"Yes, yes, yes. I'm going to see him right now," I said and hung up.

*   *   *

"What do you mean, you feel like a drink?"

"Just that, Andre. Let's go get a drink. Please, let's just go *now*!"

"Nanette, you must have caught something from Vivian. She's talking about killing a man she must know is already dead. And you—with the French police looking for us and Vivian out there with a weapon—you want to go have a nice drink somewhere."

"You got it. No more questions now, lamb-pie. Move it."

CHAPTER 15

Wham Bebop Boom Bam

I don't get it," I muttered, looking around. "Where is everybody?"

Jacques waved at us. He was the assistant manager at Bricktop's.

"*Ca va?*" he asked.

"*Oui,* I'm fine, Jacques. How come the place is so empty tonight?"

"It's Tuesday," he explained.

"Yeah, so what?"

"Everyone goes to Parker's on Tuesday. Even Monsieur Melon. Tuesday is new talent night over there. Monsieur Melon never misses new talent night at Parker's. He finds the best young musicians there and asks them to perform here. Just like you and Andre."

*   *   *

"You need help, Nan. You've lost your mind, do you know that?"

Andre was speaking through a mouthful of the chestnut crêpe that he had grabbed on the run from Bricktop's to the métro.

Parker's was back in the 5th, not ten minutes away from our place on the rue Christine.

"I can't explain it yet," I kept telling Andre. Not *all* of it. Because a couple of pieces were still missing. And without those pieces, the rest was—well, inexplicable. The important thing was to get to Parker's right away, to act now, before something irreversible happened.

When we strode through the double doors of the impeccably smoky, low-lit club, I may have looked sure of myself. I wasn't. In truth, I didn't know what was going to happen—or even *if*. Maybe Andre was right and I was loco, tripping again. But what if the evil if's stirring around up there in my brain were all true? I had to do something. This was my last chance.

A girl singer in Carmen McRae capri pants and button-down white shirt was just finishing the last chorus of "The Devil and the Deep Blue Sea."

The emcee announced intermission and a curtain of conversational babble descended, almost covering the taped music (Wayne Shorter, live, 1964) they had begun to pipe in. The voguing, profiling, and table-hopping started then. Folks moving around, floating through the place like minnows. Black-clad Euros, white Yanks with black ladies, black Yanks with blondies, and a healthy measure of prosperous Japanese in drop-dead designer clothes. Not a bad-looking crowd.

With the flummoxed Andre trailing behind me, still regarding me as if he thought I needed electroshock therapy, I made my way across the packed room to the brass-railed bar. I began to scan the crowd. If there had been any doubt before, now I knew Andre was freaked out, off his game, because I spotted the celebrated American jazz musician at a table near the stage before he did.

"What are you looking at, Nan?"

"Not 'at.' 'For.' "

"Okay. What are you looking for?"

"I'm not sure. Let's get a drink."

We ordered and I continued to look around.

"Comfortable now?" Andre was patronizing me, attempting to push me down on a barstool, a controlling hand in the small of my back.

I didn't bother to answer. I just nodded, craning my neck to take in every corner of the room.

"Boy oh boy, I hope Satchmo answers my letter," Andre said, testing me to see whether I was paying any attention to him.

I laughed and took his hand and kissed it quickly, then returned it to him.

"Who's this on the tape now," I asked, "doing 'High Fly'?"

"Jaki Byard. Like you don't know."

Andre downed a good half of his wine along with a fistful of cashews. "I never liked that guy, you know?" he said in a confessional tone, nodding discreetly toward the famous musician. "I always felt bad about it, not liking him, I mean. But I just don't. He's a smug little prick."

"Right," I said. "I'll tell you later what David Murray said about him."

Well, this was good. Andre was getting distracted from what he considered my mental breakdown. He was also getting a little drunk. Understandable, since he hadn't eaten in days. I was fighting a hunger headache of my own. He polished off the nuts and then dug in on the basket of pretzels.

"There's that couple," Andre said, pointing to an elderly man and woman not far from us. "You know, they always give us a hundred francs at Bricktop's."

"Yes, they're nice people," I agreed, not looking.

"I wonder if I should try to interview them sometime. They're not black, but they are Americans who've been over here for something like forty years. Maybe they could fill in a few blanks for me. Maybe they knew some people I can't quite nail in that chapter on the fifties."

"Good idea," I said, still searching the room. I signaled the bartender for refills.

"I guess Jacques didn't lie about all the Bricktop people being here. Those actors who always come in late are here, too," Andre noted. One of the women in the troupe was waving at us—well, at Andre. I knew what that was about. *In your dreams, bitch.*

"I bet I know what all this is about, Nan," he said a few minutes later. He was grinning like a Cheshire.

"What?" I said.

"This is some kind of complicated trick you're pulling. A surprise. For me. Somebody is about to walk in here— somebody who's so famous and so great that it's going to knock me off this chair. And you knew all along they were coming. The scene with Jacques was just part of the plan. You knew everybody'd be over here tonight because whoever's coming is going to be here tonight. I'm the only one out of the loop. Isn't that it? Some eminence is just about to walk in, and I'm going to be totally knocked out. Right?"

I looked at him. Be careful what you wish for, is what I was thinking. "Sweetie," I said, "I wish that was true."

"Then what the fuck is it, Nan? You expecting somebody from your wild past?"

"Just be patient a little longer," I begged. "Hang in there. I almost have it figured out, Andre. Have some more wine."

"No problem if you're looking for Morris," he said. "There he is—over there."

Yes. On the far side of the room Melon was holding court, as usual, the center of attention in his fraying London-tailored jacket. He and four other people were hunched around a little pin dot of a table and the old man was serving up some obviously tasty star-filled gossip. And, like always, the drinks were flowing nonstop. Lots of raucous laughter. Looked like a good time was being had by all.

Andre knocked off the guessing game for a while and began to weave this elaborate plan for making us and a number of his street music buddies famous. Something about an album featuring a miscellany of street performers playing all kinds of music. What was it he wanted to call it—*Street Smart, Street of Dreams*—something. Not a bad idea, I guess, unless somebody had already thought of it. I nodded my "that's nice, dear" approval.

"See, this wouldn't be so bad if I really was a legal resident."

"What wouldn't be so bad?" I asked.

"Your insanity. They've got socialized medicine here,

you know. We could have a shotgun wedding and I could check you directly into the clinic. Ah, Jesus, Nan, I've had it. You tell me what's going on, and tell me right now."

"Okay," I said, "I'm going to try to. But keep looking around while I'm talking."

"Look around for what, girl?"

At that very moment, my eye had fallen on a female server. Not a young person like all the others. And not wearing the ubiquitous white apron. She was walking briskly across the length of the club, tray in hand.

"The waitress—" I said slowly. I broke off there.

"What waitress?"

I grabbed his head and turned it toward the woman.

"Forget her," he said. "Why don't you ask the bartender if you want a drink?"

"No! The waitress, Andre! That woman with the tray!"

I meant the one with the automatic weapon resting next to the highball glasses. Vivian still had nice taste. She had chosen something in understated gray—very sleek, very expensive looking, and definitely not a toy.

"That's Vivian! She's going to kill him!"

I leapt off the barstool and began to rush toward Morris Melon's table. "Stop her, Andre!" I screamed as I ran. "It's Vivian! Stop her!"

Viv let the glass-laden tray fall to the floor with a crash. The important item on the tray, the gun, she was now holding with both hands as she strode like the Jolly Green Giant, closer and closer to Melon.

He and his party were so high, and so wrapped up in their own fun, they had paid no attention to the shattering glass. But now, with screams breaking out all over the place as one by one the patrons spotted Viv and realized what was happening, Melon was turning in the chair, bringing his chest full into Vivian's line of fire. He might as well have been wearing a bull's-eye on his breast.

Still a few feet away from him, I already had my arm extended so as to grab the back of his collar and pull him to the floor.

Andre was closing in on Viv using the same M.O. I heard him call her name crazily. I know she must have heard him. But she never broke stride.

The old man had bounded out of his chair before I could reach him. The others in his party were diving for cover—uselessly. Those little tin café tables wouldn't have provided decent cover for a tadpole.

The first shot rang out then, roaring past the clumsily moving Melon and exploding a glass-fronted cabinet.

Melon tried a serpentine footballer's move. Pitiful. Loping like an old dog. *Pitiful*—it was almost funny.

More screams. We were in it now.

But then, switching tactics, Melon suddenly turned back to face Vivian. He raised his arms, begging, as if a heartfelt plea was going to stop her next bullet.

Everyone seemed to freeze then, waiting for what would come next.

"Listen to me, Vivian!" Melon cried out. "I had to do it. Jerry showed up at my place. Told me he was broke, desperate. He had to have money, he said—eighty thousand dollars. I almost spat in his face. When you and Jerry took off with that hundred and fifty thousand dollars, I wanted to kill you—all of you. And now, twenty some years later, I'm supposed to bail him out of whatever trouble he's in? I laughed at him. Where was I going to get it anyway? I'd have to sell Bricktop's to raise that kind of money. But he didn't care. You know what he was like—you of all people. He said if I didn't come up with the cash, he'd start making calls—and not just to the police—he said that he'd tell—everything. I'm too old to lose everything again, Vivian. I *had* to kill him."

Vivian broke into hideous laughter. "So you had to. So what? What do I care about that? I'm glad you killed the son of a bitch. But you know this ain't about Jerry Brainard, Morris. You are *not* going to hell thinking that."

He swallowed with great effort and his eyes went neon.

"No," she stated simply. "Not for Jerry. This is for the country nigger. Isn't that what you always called him?"

Whang! went the next shot, into the amp up on stage. That caused a sort of Vietnam-movie boom that seemed to shake the club to its foundation. The people rolling around on the floor were now trying to cover their ears as well as their asses.

Melon limped on. Looking for shelter. Hollering.

Before she got off the third shot, Andre was on her. They twisted and lurched together, both of them keening and cussing as they struggled for the gun.

As I took the first step toward them, the gun began to splutter madly. I ducked, then began to crawl toward them through the bedlam.

Another burst of bullets. And then I heard Andre's roar of shocked pain.

I stood up just in time to see him go down, blood on his shirtfront.

I tried to rush Vivian, but it was no good. With a clear field now, she was aiming at Morris Melon's back, and she sent out a long, clean volley straight into him. He crumpled at the mouth of the small kitchen.

What the hell did I think I was doing? I went for her, screeching, my hands out like cat's claws.

"Get back!" she commanded, the gun now on me. "It's over, Nan. Get back!" She was shaking so hard I almost took the gamble of reaching for the weapon.

Over. How right she was.

I heard myself repeat the words I had uttered to her in the Volkswagen: "I hate you, Vivian."

Through a flood of tears she tried to say something.

I heard Andre moan deeply then, and fell on my knees beside him. When I looked up again, Vivian was disappearing through the front doors.

While the crowd scattered like frightened cockroaches, I covered Andre with my body, begging no one in particular to get help, and to let him live.

A minute or two later I heard a muffled explosion outside the walls of the café. A single burst of gunfire.

Yeah. I knew that was coming, too.

How else could something like this end?

touch her, I know I should have found some way to say

CHAPTER 16

I Want to Talk About You

I had to go. Soon. Vivian was rotting in the municipal hospital.

Luckily, I was free to suffer the agony of all the hard decisions I had to make from the relative luxury of the rue Christine. Thanks to Monsieur Simard's friend in the department, I wasn't in a jail cell on an obstruction charge.

My last look at my once-beloved aunt was a horror show in itself. She lay all curled into herself on the stones out behind the kitchen of Parker's. Most of her face was gone. Deal with that. I'd never seen anything worse. Yet all I could think was: My God, how little she looks—she must be so lonely. But, touch her? No. Nuh-uh. She was family, my father's flesh and blood; she and I had loved each other once; and I knew I'd forgive her someday for all the pain and mayhem she had caused. But I would not touch her. I know I should have found some way to say good-bye to her. I guess I could have prayed over her, or something, but I didn't. I was stupefied by then and I had to get to the hospital to be with Andre.

They found a letter addressed to me in Viv's skirt pocket. But not the ten thousand dollars. The message, written on the back of a café menu, was less a suicide note than a cryptic, telegraphic kind of poem:

Nanette—
Forgive all the lies. But that's what liars do. So now I've got only one truth to give you. Six months ago. In Chicago. Down and out. As usual. Trying to figure a way out. As usual. I've got a job not worth having and a man not worth the trouble—but a damn sight better than me. They tell me over at the clinic I got cancer and nothing they can do about it. Nothing I can do rather.

A lot of thinking about it all. Everything I did and everything I didn't do. My father. Your father. Jerry and the rest of the stupid parade. Out of all of them, only one really loved me. And that was the one I betrayed. He never did make up his mind what side of the fence he should be playing on. But that didn't matter. I always knew he loved me. Traveling Viv, always on the move. I say to myself, Girl, it's time for one last trip before Miss Cancer comes by for tea. Time to make amends.

You'll never look up to me again baby. But please don't look down on me either. I love you Nan and I'm sorry.

One of our street musician acquaintances had brought a keyboard by the apartment. Andre sat up in bed for hours on end picking out tunes on it with one hand. He was going to be just fine. Andre did not appreciate being told that his wound was not particularly "serious," and in his place neither would I. After all, getting *shot* is by definition serious when it's your body the bullet has ripped through. But he did need to let the wound near his left nipple heal. Playing the violin would have to wait for at least a month. There was no reason he couldn't go outside if he took it easy, though . . . walk, sit in the café. He just didn't want to.

I fed him soup and gave him his antibiotics and, as if I weren't already guilty enough, broke his heart all over again every time we argued about me going back to New York. That argument seemed to take up about twenty out of every twenty-four hours. In the heat of the moment he called me a few names I knew he didn't mean, and so I never responded in kind.

"Look, Andre! I know you're deep into being Mr. Black Paris Exile. But for god's sake, baby, even Sidney Bechet came home once in a while—didn't he?"

"Stop calling it home, Nan."

"But it is!"

"Bullshit. Home is someplace where you belong. Where you're wanted, and respected, and loved. Unconditionally. Home is where there's a place for you."

"I have a place for you, idiot. I have a home for you. We can work, Andre. We can get back here."

"To visit, you mean." He said it as though there was spoiled milk in his mouth. "Dabble, you mean. That's not me, Nanette. I'm not into vacationing. I want to belong. I'm for real."

"And I'm not? Just because I can see it's my place to take Viv's body home—be with my parents over this. I not only let her die alone, I threw away ten thousand dollars, man! I couldn't turn away from Viv while she was alive, and I can't turn away now."

"But from me you can. Right?"

"But I don't want to, Andre. I don't want to."

"Well, you have to. Understand that. You have to either turn away from her or turn away from me."

After a while he just stopped talking. He put on a pair of blue-tinted wire-rim shades that just covered his eyeballs, and sat there looking like a banjie-boy CIA operative.

I tried to play it for laughs. I tried reasoning with him. I tried to play it from every angle in the book. But he wasn't having it. I was "leaving him," that's how he saw it. "Leaving. Period." The silent treatment became his way of leaving me before I left him.

I knew how miserable he was. Because I knew how miserable I was.

When Inspector Simard phoned to say he was in Paris and wanted us to join him for lunch, I begged Andre to get dressed and come. But he wouldn't budge.

"I'm bringing back some ice cream for you," I told him as I slipped on my shoes and picked up the folding umbrella. "What flavor do you want? Pistachio?"

No answer.

"Come on, sweetheart. Please come. Simard wants to see you. He asked for you especially."

Nothing.

"You really hate me now, huh, Geechee? Okay. Pistachio it is."

Ile St. Louis in the rain. Notre Dame hanging behind me in the mist like the fingers of an old hand pointing blackly up at God. There was a time when that would have given the old tear ducts a workout. All out of tears now. Well, there would be plenty of time for that later. Never made love with Andre while it was raining. How could that be?

Simard looked very snappy in his dark suit. He stood as I approached the table, took my hands into his, looked into my eyes for a long time. For a minute there I thought he might kiss me. But no, he was an elderly man who had seen me only twice in his life and that Gallic sense of reserve was too strong. Still, I took note of the kindness in his eyes and was grateful for it.

I extended a fake apology on Andre's behalf for his absence, and the meal commenced. The inspector of course did all the ordering. The food was beautiful and we put off talking about the very reason he and I had ever crossed paths until the waiter was clearing away the dishes.

"So," he said, "I have seen a copy of the letter your aunt left for you. The anguish in it was painfully apparent. It must have been heartbreaking for you to read."

I nodded.

"At any rate, the autopsy has confirmed what she told you. She was indeed gravely ill. There was an inoperable cancer of the pancreas. One of the worst sorts, I'm told." He stopped there, but a minute later added, "I've always said, when the day comes that I'm given a similar diagnosis, I will most certainly consider her way of . . ."

"Going out," I said, in English. "Yes, me too, I think. But in a much quieter way."

I took a long drink from my—what?—third glass of wine. "It's been mighty quiet lately in the apartment. I've had plenty of time these past few days to try out a lot of answers to everything that happened.

"When Vivian was holding Andre and me in that car, she told us a series of lies. But, in her own crazy way, she was telling the truth at the same time. What I mean is, she laid out the cast of characters, and she provided a list of their actions—their betrayals, if you will. What I had to do was juggle the players—switch the names and faces and match them with the crimes committed.

"I think I know what happened to all the players, including my aunt. I don't claim it's the whole story, but it's close enough to explain almost everything—almost."

"Please," Simard said. "I am eager to hear it."

I began. "The time is more than twenty years ago. Vivian is young and gorgeous, and all the players are having the time of their lives. Americans in Paris. Vivian, Jerry, Morris Melon, and Ez. Morris Melon and Ez hit on a scam to make money. Surely Melon was the mastermind for the scheme. Vivian may or may not have been in on the planning of the scam. I say she wasn't; I say Ez was indiscreet and leaked to her what Melon and he were planning to do. That would be perfectly understandable, because Ez was flipping from Morris Melon's bed to Vivian's. Unable to decide which side of the fence he was playing, in Vivian's words. Let's say that little Ez was quite drunk with being desired by this sexy lady *and* this very smart, sophisticated, charismatic older man.

"So now Vivian knows about the scheme. And she tells Jerry about it. Jerry takes it all in, and bides his time to see if Ez and Melon can really pull such a thing off.

"Well, what do you know? It appears to be working. Ez is posing as this blues singer and songwriter from the South with the disingenuous moniker of Little Rube Haskins. He's making a splash in Europe with his songs. Except they aren't his songs. They're tunes stolen from old compilations of folk music gathered by historians nearly half a century before.

"Now, Inspector, here I have to add a footnote to this story that jumps from the present to the past and back again. My friend Andre is a kind of walking archive. Never forgets a thing. But for some reason his memory betrayed him when it came to Morris Melon. Andre knew that he'd heard Melon's name in connection to some kind of scholarship related to the migration of blacks from the South to the North. But he had the story just a little bit wrong. Melon was a scholar all right, a sociologist, but his great interest was in music, and he had taken part in one of the song-gathering missions to the South in the 1940s. I've also had time to make a phone call to a music critic friend back in New York. He found Melon's name and even his photograph in the literature accompanying some of the old recordings. Melon himself had some musical talent, and it was easy for him to take those songs and rework the tunes and lyrics. He and Ez would have been exposed in no time back in the States, but over here it was a different story.

"So, to pick up with the Ez and Vivian story, it seems

he's decided at last which side of the fence he wants. He's now head over heels in love with her. And she makes him think she loves him, too. But she's married to Jerry Brainard."

"Not really," Simard said, shaking his head. "No record of a marriage between them has ever surfaced."

"I see. Yet another one of Vivian's lies. Well, no matter. Married or not, she wasn't planning to leave Jerry. And, probably at Jerry's direction, she played Ez for everything he was worth and got her hands on his money. She cleans him out, gets the money to Jerry, and then, in keeping with the plans that she and Jerry have made, she runs.

"Vivian waits for Jerry. And waits. But he doesn't show and he doesn't send for her. Slowly it begins to dawn on her that he never will. Meanwhile, poor Ez is brutally murdered. Vivian hears about it. She thinks that Jerry ran out on her *and* killed Little Rube.

"Now you come onstage, Inspector. You take the murder seriously, pursue what leads you have. But, unfortunately, the police never catch the killer.

"The one and only winner in this story: Jerry Brainard. The murdering bastard has double-crossed everyone. Vivian and Melon can do nothing. For obvious reasons, they can't tell the authorities, or anyone else, a thing. Besides that, they don't even know where the hell Jerry is.

"Curtain on the Little Rube Haskins story. No recordings exist to carry on his legend. A few people know who he was, but in general he's merely a footnote to a footnote in music history.

"The years pass. Morris Melon becomes a kind of elder statesman of the smart black set in Paris. Mister

Bon Vivant. It's like he got a second chance. Life didn't turn out so bad for him after all.

"Jerry Brainard, according to you, Monsieur Simard, becomes a career criminal, if not a terribly successful one. A little hijacking, a little smuggling, maybe a gofer for some of the more powerful criminals. Still, he manages to stay out of prison.

"Vivian gets on with her life, too. If we buy her story, she's been bumming around for the past fifteen years or so and the party, as she said, is finally over. Vivian is now older, and bitter, and sick. She hears that Jerry Brainard, the man who used her and deserted her, is living in Paris. And knowing she's going to die soon, she decides to exact a belated revenge, not just for herself but for Ez. Somehow she scrapes together the money to get here.

"Only Brainard always seems to be a few steps ahead of her. He seems to know where to find her before she knows where to find him. When someone comes around to her hotel to try to kill her, she assumes it was Jerry who sent him. She's so spooked that she never returns to her room. Finally, Viv is horrified when Brainard kills a woman, one of his criminal colleagues, and implicates her in the murder. It appears that Jerry is systematically planting evidence against her. She's in a rage now. She's going to get him if it's the last thing she ever does in this world.

"Then something truly unexpected happens. One day Vivian hears from one of her low-life sources that a young woman who claims to be her niece from New York is looking for her. She wants to know what on earth I'm doing here, why I'm trying to find her. Maybe it's a trap. But just maybe the family's worried about her and I've been sent to bail her out—which of course happened to be exactly right. But she can't just walk up to me and Andre. She's in danger, she's being hunted. So she stakes us out. She stalks us for a while.

"Viv is broke by now, desperate. Her last few dollars are back at the hotel, and she can't go back there. But if I do happen to have money for her, she wants it. No conditions. No questions asked. When she gets the opportunity, she forces Andre at gunpoint into this old heap she's gotten from god knows who or where. She makes him tell her about my mission here, and then holds the gun on him while he calls me to come and ransom him back.

"Big confession in the back seat of the Volkswagen. Big lies, rather. But are they?"

"Now," he said, lighting my cigarette as well as his own, "I think I see where you are going with this story. What your aunt told you in the car was both true and false. She did indeed intend to kill this man from her past. To obtain her revenge. But by the time of her confession to you, this man was no longer Jerry Brainard. She was planning to kill Monsieur Melon."

"That's right, Inspector. Melon was her target. And she was his.

"Vivian gets over here, intent on killing Jerry, but before she can do much of anything, Jerry is murdered. And it is that murder that leads to the subsequent revelation of who murdered Rube Haskins.

"Viv figures out that it was Morris Melon who killed Jerry Brainard, or had him killed. And suddenly she knows—it was Melon who murdered Ez, too. As you pointed out, there was hatred and passion behind that crime. Who would strike the victim like that and then run

over him again and again until there was nothing left—
Jerry? No. He was obviously no prize in the morality department. But Vivian's affair with Ez meant nothing to
him. But Morris Melon? Not only didn't he get his share
of the money from Ez, he was spurned by him as a lover
as well. My God, I would think that if Melon could have
gotten his hands on Vivian he'd have killed her as well."

"Melon," he confirmed. "Of course, Melon. But how
did your aunt come so quickly to the conclusion that
Monsieur Melon was Jerry Brainard's murderer?"

"It was the Mary Polk murder that convinced her. She
read, just as Andre and I did, that the police had questioned and released a small-time criminal named Gigi
Lacroix. One of the papers carried a photograph of him.
Vivian recognized him immediately as the man who tried
to kill her that day in the hotel. She assumed when Gigi
first attacked her that he was Jerry's goon. But by the
time of the Mary Polk murder, Jerry was already dead.
She knew that it had to be Morris Melon who was after
her; that Gigi worked for him, not Jerry. From there, it
wasn't much of a leap to realize Morris Melon was responsible for Ez's death, too. And so it was still payback
time, but not for Jerry. For Melon.

"But of course Nanette and her young man Andre don't
know any of that. They walk right into the old man's net.
He befriends them, sets them up with a part-time gig in his
place, where he can track their progress just by keeping
his ears open.

"And who has little Nanette enlisted to help find her
aunt? A small-time criminal who knows a little bit about
a lot of things. Gigi Lacroix. The very hood who works

as a strong-arm man, snitch, or whatever, for Morris Melon.

"Lacroix appreciated so many of life's little ironies. He was taking money from me for the same service that Melon was paying him for—finding Vivian. 'Just string her along,' Melon probably told him. 'Take the money she gives you and tell her as little as possible.'

"There was more irony than I knew what to do with, Inspector. For instance—yes, somebody was framing her with those items from her suitcase, but it wasn't Jerry; it was Morris Melon. His man Gigi must have gotten his hands on Viv's address book. Melon sent that telegram asking for money, hoping somebody from the family would come over here and flush Vivian out. It was just a long shot for him. Little did he know, I actually did have a jackpot for her.

"And then there was all Viv's talk about betrayal. But the terrible betrayal wasn't Jerry's betrayal of her; it was her betrayal of Ez. She put the knife in Ez. On and on."

Simard was doing his duty as taster as the waiter opened yet another bottle of wine. He nodded his approval and our glasses were filled. We drank in silence for a time.

"I know how useless hindsight is," I commented later. "But, thinking back on everything, I realize how plain some of these things should have been to me. Staring me in the face, almost. Once Andre played that cassette, the apples weren't just falling off the branches, they were practically jumping into the basket.

"But they were all jumbled together, see. I couldn't untangle all the parts of Vivian's story yet. It was impossible to sort out fact from fantasy, or just plain lies. But I knew Melon had to be at the center of everything. Old Satan.

"*Big* mistake, my not picking up on that one. Should have known immediately that day in the Volkswagen that when Vivian used that strange phrase she was referring to Melon and not Jerry. But, you know, here's the thing about Old Satan Melon: it's as if he made the decision to be as evil as he possibly could be. He made himself into a Satan. I mean, he must have started out on the side of the angels, and then, once he slipped—pulled that fraud with Rube Haskins—he figured he had to go all the way to the other end of morality—to being a devil. I remember how he talked about the blessedness of black people from the country. *Grace* was the word he used. When he hatched that scheme, it was like he was stealing the grace from his people and renouncing his own blessedness. He must have been so profoundly ashamed of what he'd done that he had to kill everyone who knew about it. He wasn't just killing people, he was killing his shame. First Ez. Then Jerry. Mary Polk. Then Vivian, very nearly. And finally Gigi, who had been Melon's hired assassin."

"Yes," Simard said. "In light of what your aunt said, Melon surely dispatched Lacroix to kill her. But as for the others? Open to question, I would say. With a little planning, Monsieur Melon might very well have personally carried out the murders of Mary Polk and Brainard. And he no doubt killed Lacroix. There is a very likely scenario based on what you reported to the police: The night of Gigi's death, Monsieur Melon was ill, or pretended to be ill with a hangover. He retired to his private office to sleep. But, while you and Andre and the others performed, he simply made the short walk to the métro, joined Lacroix in the square, sat quite close to him as they talked, and soundlessly drove the knife into his body. He returned to Bricktop's, slipped in by the back entrance, and no one was any the wiser."

"Right. That is how I'd figure it."

"As to why he felt he must get rid of Lacroix at that moment? We cannot be certain. Either Lacroix simply knew too much about his deeds, or Melon suspected that Lacroix was on the verge of trying to sell you some real information for a change—something that was much too dangerous for you to know."

"The thing is, Inspector, what made him start down that road in the first place? All the way back to the scam with Ez, I mean. What kind of pressure could have caused Morris Melon to sell out his principles so completely?

"In fact, that's what I can't figure out about all the people in this singular group of—I don't know what to call them—displaced persons—expatriates. For the moment let's call them that. Why did they do those stupid, stupid things? What sort of forces, mysteries, were driving them?

"I asked my aunt a question as she was driving away. 'What do you need that money for?' Viv knew she didn't have a chance of getting away after killing Melon. She didn't answer me then, and now those money orders have vanished. What did she do with them? What? God knows, I'd love to be able to answer that question when my mother asks it.

"As for Jerry Brainard, you know what I'm starting to believe about him, Inspector? Bad guy that he was? That he once cared for Vivian almost as much as she did for him. That he was a weak guy, always in trouble, always in debt, and he talked her into getting that money from Ez because right then it was the simplest way to get what he needed. I wonder if he didn't eventually realize he'd have been better off staying with Viv and working for a living like everybody else."

Simard smiled ruefully. "And what about Haskins?" he said. "What was, in your estimation, his driving need?"

"His need was for Vivian, I suppose. Poor bastard."

"Poor bastard," the inspector echoed. "You've cast a very forgiving eye on all the players in your little drama, you know. Mysteries or no mysteries, I could never look at them with the kind of pity you do. But, tell me this: are you purposely leaving one character out of this complicated tale of expatriates?"

"Who would that be?"

"Yourself, my friend."

Me? Sure, I could toss around some ideas about what drives me. But I did much better speculating, piecing together the motivations of four dead people. Who weren't around to tell me I was full of shit.

I merely shrugged.

We'd been lunching for three and a half hours. I had to get back to the rue Christine.

"I take it," Monsieur Simard said as I walked him to his taxi, "that you and Andre . . ." He allowed his voice to simply drop off the cliff there.

I shook my head, not trusting myself to speak.

"Ah." That was all he said. But the word seemed to come from his chest.

"Nanette," he said a few minutes later. It startled me. It was the first time he had called me by my first name.

"Oui?"

"You loved your aunt, did you not? And you believe that, despite the unhappy turn her life took, she loved you as well?"

I nodded.

"I think, Nanette, you must accept that everyone is entitled to his mysteries. But perhaps there is a very practical answer to what Vivian did with the bulk of that ten thousand dollars."

I looked at him expectantly.

"If Rube Haskins was so completely taken in by her, he probably told her who he really was. She may have known his real name, where he was born, everything."

"Yes, that makes sense."

"What was that phrase you used . . . payback? Too little, and too late. But a kind of payback." He continued to look benignly at me.

"What is it you're not telling me, Monsieur Simard?"

"The clerk who sold postage to your aunt remembered her because she looked ill. As if she had a fever. After she left you and Andre standing in Cité Prost, your aunt Vivian sent a large envelope by air to the United States. That is all the young lady at the post office recalled."

Ah. So maybe Vivian had made a last-ditch attempt to redress the wrong she had done Ez. She had sent her inheritance to his family.

I kissed the inspector then. I couldn't help myself. "I'll write to you," I said.

"Excellent. I haven't had a good letter in ten years."

"And will you?" I asked.

"The minute anything interesting occurs."

*   *   *

I forgot the ice cream.
Just as well.
Andre was gone.

Nan:
Go. Leave keys downstairs. Go Go I won't come back
till you do.

I packed in a hurry, to say the least, so I'm sure I must
have left something behind. If so, I didn't do it on pur-
pose. Believe me.

Yes, I thought, there was another cue I hadn't picked
up on. Before I left the apartment to join Simard, Andre
was playing around with that keyboard. He was playing
at something kitschy—Viennese—something like "Fasci-
nation." But, as I descended the stairs, I could have sworn
I heard the opening notes to Gordon Jenkins's "Good-
bye."

CHAPTER 17

Parting Is Not Good-bye

I wrote a note, too. On the back of the one he'd left for me. But in the end I didn't leave it.

I had it in my purse.

What am I doing here?

I belonged with Andre, didn't I? He was the one who was so caught up with "belonging" to a place. Not me, not anymore. I was beginning to accept that I'd always be a little bit on the periphery. Fuck the *place*—it was Andre I belonged with, no? So what was I doing up above the world, heading back to America? Alone.

You're taking Vivian's body home. That's what you're doing. Her brother is going to bury her, and maybe you along with her.

To repeat, I belonged with Andre, didn't I? Here was a man who had not only pledged the rest of his life to me. Not only could play "Billie's Bounce" on the violin. Not only showed a willingness to face down my shitty karma.

He loved me enough to take a bullet that by all rights should have been mine.

"*Madame?*" I heard a soft voice say.

The flight was only half full. The attendant with the chignon wouldn't leave me alone. I had already declined the game hen dinner, smoked salmon, honey peanuts, champagne, the current issue of *Paris Vogue*, and the in-flight Julia Roberts movie. With each offer I turned my puffy, ugly old face to her and tried to answer in the fewest polite French words possible.

I had downed an ocean of black coffee since boarding the plane.

The poison gas began to rise again in my stomach as I had another flashback of Vivian lying in that alley with the back of her head blown off.

I turned on the overhead light to help chase the image away.

I lived too much in the past. That was my trouble. That's what the music was about, when you really got down to it. It wasn't just what I did for a half-assed living, what I respected and loved. It was my escape from the world as presently constituted.

Worse, it wasn't even *my* past. All my life it seems I've been caught up with the people, the music, and the feel of life at another time, a time at least three generations removed from my own. Here you are, little Nanette, it's 1969 and here's the gift of life. Welcome to the world, dear. What are you going to be, a postal worker, a bank manager—you know, they let us do that kind of thing now—or a computer whiz? *Me? Thanks, but no thanks. I'd rather be Mary Lou Williams. Ivy Anderson? Or, yeah, how about Sonny Rollins?* I could never get with the music I was supposed to like. Nor the kind of man I was supposed to like. Nor the kind of ambitions that were supposed to drive me forward. I don't give a damn about the things that excite or tie up the folks drinking shooters on the Upper West Side or hanging with Spike in Fort Greene.

Yes, through the music of the past I had, like Andre, found a way to honor my forefathers. But I knew there was something terribly dishonest about the way I lived. It wasn't just living in a fantasy world, it wasn't just being phony—it was wrong. It's wrong not to live in the here and now. It's cowardly and pious and arrogant and wrong.

And the other kids just don't like me.

If I played my cards right I could spend the whole flight beating up on myself. I think it must have been Ernestine, that voice in my ear, that was telling me: *If you feel this awful, you must deserve it.*

Pictures of Andre were now interspersed with the memories of Vivian. Those big feet of his, and the way he moved, and that hollow place in his lower back. The day he took me on that breathless guided tour, the same day we first went to Bricktop's. Teasing him then, I said he was crazy—that his devotion to the past had crazed him. Well, maybe that was no joke; maybe he *was* crazy, crazy for real. And, finally, those cold blue killer-for-hire shades that had obscured his eyes, hidden him, taken him from me during the last days we had together.

Belong with him? said Ernestine scornfully. *You'll never see him again.*

It wasn't fair, it wasn't fair.

I dug a few paper napkins out of the seat-back pocket and dabbed at my eyes.

Would Andre continue to live and work in Paris, stay on in France forever? He sure had the talent and the determination. I had no doubt he would do our forebears proud, the obscure ones along with the famous. All those black people with a hyperdeveloped sense of the romantic which takes them to faraway places, out of the here and now they were born to endure in America. Maybe someday, as maturity softened his contempt, he'd be able to view Little Rube Haskins in a more sympathetic light. And Morris Melon. And me. All us permanent strangers.

Sure, Andre would distinguish himself in print or as a venerable lecturer or an acclaimed performer. He'd get— I made myself say it—get married, become a French citizen, like he wanted, and grow into his Inspector Simard role. A stone cottage in the provinces, two dogs—the whole bit. *Un homme français.*

The aircraft shimmied a little and then the pilot's reassuring baritone issued from the loudspeaker. In a nutshell: *Go back to sleep, it's going to be okay.*

Would I ever see Paris again? Probably. It was unbearable to think of dying without seeing those lights once more. Would I ever cry again as I drove past the Arc de Triomphe or walked in the Bois du Boulogne? Maybe. Would I ever again feel that the city belonged to me, and I to it? Like I wasn't just another savvy tourist, or even a starry-eyed expatriate, but the genuine article—*une femme française.*

No.

Please turn this page
for a
bonus excerpt

DRUMSTICKS

a humorous ... ... latte
available
wherever books are sold.

It's Magic

This fucking thing does *not* work! I thought bitterly.

I was pretty grim that afternoon. Two days since Justin had given me the Mama Lou doll and I was damned if I could see any magic changes taking place in my life.

So much for voodoo. So much for Perry Mason.

I had the doll propped up in my saxophone case, so that she could oversee and bless those bills raining into the case as the public showed its grateful appreciation for my playing. Ha. The previous day's take had been mediocre. Today's was downright lousy.

I was blowing in the Times Square station, where any number of musicians I knew from the scene told me they'd been cleaning up as of late. The pickings were supposed to be ripe in Times Square now, owing in great part to the Disneyfication of the area. Hordes

1

of out-of-towners roamed there freely, taking the subways by day and night, no longer afraid of being held up, raped, carjacked, and so on. Little by little, New York is getting rehabilitated as a tourist mecca—that is, becoming a shopping mall, where the real Americans can feel at home.

Like all dyed-in-the-wool Manhattanites, I found the so-called clean-up of 42nd Street distasteful. What with the pimps, the porn movie houses, the touts for the live sex shows, the drugs, the parasites that hung around the Port Authority terminal, and all the rest of that scuzz, the old 42nd Street had been no picnic. But it was preferable to this version of Wonderland where everybody was buying inflatable Little Mermaids and queuing up for *The Lion King*.

I had had it with the Deuce, as they were calling Times Square in the seventies. I threw in the towel: packed up and rode up to street level on the spanking new escalator.

I'd locked Mama Lou inside the case with a cruel little laugh, hoping she'd suffocate in there.

I walked east, stopping at the main library on Fifth Avenue. I slipped into Bryant Park and crunched around on a few dead leaves, sat down on one of the benches for fifteen minutes or so. Then I went back out onto the pavement to try my luck playing again. Once more I propped up old Mama Lou, my supposed lucky charm.

I got a couple of bucks from some student types, a fiver from a European couple, and assorted coins from the sainted New York types who seem to give money automatically to anybody who asks for it.

After a couple of hours I headed downtown on foot, thinking evil thoughts about the corn-fed tourists in their K Mart jeans; the mayor and his fucking gated-community mind-set; lite jazz; turn-off notices; autumn in New York; my bloody karma; and, especially, Mama Lou.

I needed to stop off for groceries. Given the current budget, spaghetti sounded delicious. In the supermarket I walked past the lamb chops and straight to the pasta aisle.

At home, I looked at the Jack Daniel's bottle but didn't go for it. Instead I kicked out of my shoes and opened a beer. While I made supper, I listened to a Lady Day/Lester tape I've always been fond of, going over to the machine a couple of times to replay "This Year's Kisses."

My tough guy pose had pretty much dissolved, helped along by that titanic crying fit the other day. I was beginning to feel a little more like myself, kind of human. But I was still broke and I was still sad.

No rush to hear my phone messages. What was the point? I had little desire to talk to anyone. Unless it was Aubrey, I did not plan to return the call. But, just before turning in, I did press the message button and listen.

The voice, a woman's, was vaguely familiar. Not until she said something about a $350 check did I recognize the voice to be that of the secretary at the travel magazine where I work periodically, translating articles from French into English. Apparently, through some computer mix-up, they had the wrong address for me. They had been sending me the same check, and getting it back in the mail, for weeks.

Money! At last, a piece of good luck.

I sent up a little prayer of thanks and a silent apology to Justin. If he had such great faith in the silly doll, then I guess I could give her a little credit, too.

Actually, Mama Lou was not the first doll I owned as an adult. I used to keep some little West African cuties on a shelf in the kitchen, but I ditched them when I last repainted the apartment—ended up giving them to a neighbor's little girl.

I used to tell all my secrets to my dolly when I was a kid. In fact, if memory serves, my father caught me whispering tearfully to her once. Naturally he insisted on knowing what I was telling her. I'm sure I lied to him. Daddy wasn't big on superstitions or black people who fell under their sway. Lucky charms, Friday the 13th, dream books, avoiding ladders and cracks in the sidewalk. All nonsense, he said. Work hard, eat right, do the honorable thing, and you won't need luck.

But I did. I needed a lucky break.

Four days a week, the north quadrant of Union Square Park was converted into a farmers market— a heady mix of ravishing wildflowers, spices, craft works, and seasonal produce. Twenty varieties of apples and squash and arcane hybrids of potatoes; pumpkins as big as a Volkswagen, homemade pies, sheepskin blankets, and brick oven focaccia; hand-churned butter and organic honey—an endless list of goods that city folks craved and were prepared to pay dearly for. By night, the same patch of the park became a gathering place for teenagers polishing their rollerblading skills.

So, the question was, Did I really need that bunch of authentic, gritty broccoli rabe, or was I inventing an errand just so I could get a look at the doll's creator, the real-life Mama Lou?

With the bustling market on my left, I walked and scanned the skinny strip of Broadway—or Union Square West, as the new street sign was calling it—running along the park. There was a vitamin store at the corner of 17th, and next to it, a McDonald's. I'd always found that kind of amusing.

A few doors below, there was a pissy-looking wine shop, and then the terraced seafood restaurant where middle-aged lovers liked to gather on summer nights.

I continued south. Past the hugely successful all-night coffee shop where the younger crowd flocked, naively hoping to spot a few supermodels consuming their midday yogurt and heroin.

Finally, 15th Street. That was where the dolls were sold, Justin had said. I'll be damned, there they were! A bevy of dark dolls dressed in riotous colors. The folding table, set up in front of the office building with a bank on the ground floor, was thick with them. And the real Mama Lou was at her place, on a metal chair. No customers around, she was playing solitaire at one edge of the table.

I didn't go up to her right away. Instead I looked at the goods on the unattended folding table next to hers, which contained a sea of unctuous body musk in dark little glass vials. Some people find those scents sexy, I think. I don't get that.

"He'll be back in a minute, honey," the doll lady said, placing a ten of hearts on the jack of spades. "I'm watching his stuff for him."

"Oh, that's okay," I said. "I'm just looking."

A black man with matted hair, who had been dozing near the entrance to the ATM, roused himself and approached me, paper cup extended.

I gave him a buck, but when he wanted to engage me in one of those panhandler flirtations, I shook him off and sauntered over to the doll lady's table.

"What's the matter?" she said with a teasing laugh. "Don't you need a new boyfriend?"

"Funny you should ask," I said. "As a matter of fact, I do. Since I can't get the old one back."

"Oh, you'll get him, honey. Just let me know if his granddaddy is single."

We had a good laugh together.

"What's your name, baby?" she said.

"Nan."

"I'm Ida Williams."

She swept all the cards together then, ending the game. I looked at her ebony hands, nimble even though they were old, with knuckles like little marbles.

"You've got some worries on your mind, huh?" she said.

I was taken aback. "Does it show?"

She didn't answer.

"I guess I haven't been having the best luck lately with—well, with anything."

6

"Um hum. Well, that's going to change, baby."

"You think so?"

"Everything in its time, honey, everything in its time."

Mrs. Williams patted my hand then. I was crying, and I hadn't even known it.

Three young women laden with shopping bags walked up to the table just then. A lucky thing that they did. Because otherwise I might have unloaded my worried mind on Mrs. Williams. Which would have been incredibly dumb. I'd known the woman for all of five minutes. There was just so much empathy in those old eyes of hers. She was friendly and funny and salty. But, oddly enough, there seemed to be sadness in her as well.

The potential customers began examining Ida's wares. She went into her spiel and I stepped aside.

"Nice to meet you," I called to her as I began to walk away.

"All right, you have a beautiful day, honey."

I looked back, more than a little skeptical.

"Just look up," she added. "See? It's already beautiful, isn't it?"

She was right. I removed my scarf and let the strong sun play on the back of my neck. It felt wonderful.

I could do no wrong.

Yesterday was yesterday. Today, I could do no wrong. Or should I say "we" could do no wrong. The Mama Lou doll sat there beaming with pride while I played my ass off.

I had planned to play outside the big soulless café on 53rd Street and Seventh Avenue for only an hour or so and then head back downtown. But the crowd wouldn't let me go. The case was fat with dollar bills.

One nattily dressed older man, hammered on martinis by the smell of things, had me play "Save Your Love for Me" three times. With every rendition he would drop another ten-dollar bill. When he was young, he said, he had a terrible crush on Nancy Wilson. He was staying at the Sheraton, which was just across the street, by the way, if I was interested.

Then a lady in a fur asked if I knew Stevie Wonder's "Ribbon in the Sky." Not really. I bumbled my way through it. Ten bucks from her, too.

Your girl was money that day.

I finally did close up shop, put the loot in my wallet, and walk to the nearest station for the downtown Lex.

Maybe I ought to buy Mama Lou a fur, I thought as the train whipped along. Keep her warm all through the winter.

At the 23rd Street station I took the stairs two at a time. And practically floated up the stairs to my apartment.

That night's phone message beat the one from the magazine by a mile: my old music coach, Jeff Moses, was phoning to say he had a regular gig for me, if I wanted it. I would be filling in for an ailing saxophonist, part of a trio that played three nights a week at a restaurant uptown.

Damn right I wanted it.

I ran over to my instrument case, tore Mama Lou from her prison, and gave her a big wet kiss.

"Good afternoon, Mrs. Williams." I greeted the thin, dark-skinned woman wearing a red windbreaker over her brightly patterned dress.

"How you today, honey?" she answered with a smile.

"I'm fine. Much better. And I just wanted to thank you."

She furrowed her brow.

"Let me explain," I said. "A friend of mine gave me one of your dolls a few days ago. Like you said, I've had a lot of worries. But my luck has totally changed."

"Well, of course," she said. "These dolls have got some powers, girl. Powers we don't even know about."

"I'm sure you're right, Mrs. Williams. And by the way, do you make all these yourself?"

"Just call me Ida. Yes, I make them. Each one is different, see, just like us. But they all have the power. And I'll tell you something else about 'em, baby. They only work when you ready for them to work. So you musta been ready."

As she talked, she was subtly moving a couple of the dolls forward on the table surface. "Of course, some are a little more special than others. Look at this one here."

"She's beautiful," I said, "and she looks like she means business, too."

"She" was a tall and lanky black one—a kind of mamba priestess in an intense blue sarong and orange headdress. There was a circle of wire at her neck

9

and she wore an ankle bracelet. She, too, carried a little medicine pouch.

Ida picked up the doll and pressed her into my hands. "Now I'm not saying the one you have can't bring you what you need to be happy. But with this one, honey, you could rule the world."

Quite a claim.

I had been playing my belief in Mama Lou for laughs, more or less. Even Justin's credence seemed a bit tongue-in-cheek.

Was it possible that Ida's faith in her creations was the real thing—that she actually believed what she was saying?

"How much?" I asked.

"She's a really special one, remember. But for you . . . eighteen-fifty."

Ida couldn't possibly support herself by selling these, I was thinking; I mean, realistically, even on the best day, how big is the demand for voodoo picaninnies? But on the other hand, she was a very smooth saleswoman. If she was able to play everybody else as deftly as she was handling me—well, maybe there was enough in it to cover the rent.

I pulled a twenty from my money belt and told her to keep the change.

"You are a sweet thing," she crooned. "Just you wait and see what kinds of good things are gon' come to you."

I was halfway across the park. But then I turned back and ran over to her table again. "I want to invite you someplace, Ida. I'd like you to come as my guest."

"Me? Where you want to invite me?"

"To hear me play. You like music, don't you?"

"Do I look like I don't? We wouldn't be nothing without music."

I wrote down the address of the restaurant where my three-day-a-week gig was to take place and told Ida I would leave her name with the host up front.

"This sounds like a pretty fancy place."

I shrugged and made a motion with my hand that signified "Don't worry about it."

"That's okay with me, girl. I got a dress that'll knock 'em out."

I laughed. "Cool, Ida. I can't wait to see it."

"What kind of music you play—piano?"

"No. Sax. I'm in this trio."

"Lord, if that don't beat all. I bet your mama and daddy real proud of you. Will they be there?" she asked.

I smiled. "Not this time."

I put the second doll in my case, so that Mama Lou wouldn't be lonely. I just hoped she wouldn't be jealous.

I took pains, usually, to avoid Soho.

But I did have that $350 windfall, and the restaurant where I was going to be playing was kind of grown-up/dress-up, and there was that one nice shop on Prince Street that sold some of the world's greatest black skirts—black chiffon skirts with lace overlays; black wool skirts slit up to where even your doctor shouldn't be looking; ballgown-length black taffeta skirts; tight ones, long ones, short ones. I like them all. So when I left Ida, I set off straight down Broadway to find something to wear to the gig.

My luck was holding. I even found a quarter on the ground.

I didn't hang on to it for very long, though. Before I reached 8th Street, an aged, pitiful-looking drag queen with big old feet hit me for money. It didn't even occur to me not to comply. I gave her the quarter and all the rest of the change I had in my pockets.

I was getting arrogant—spreading my good luck around.

Repetition

The audience at Omega, an upscale eatery way up on First Avenue, came primarily to eat, not to hear the music. Jeff had told me that from the git. But the clientele was too sophisticated to treat us as mere white noise; there would be plenty of diners who knew the difference between elevator jazz and the real deal.

In other words, it was unlikely I was going to be discovered and whisked into the recording studio by the kind of scout who haunts the neighborhood basketball courts or the comedy clubs looking for fresh meat. But I did have to have my stuff together to play with the consummate professionals who were to be my fellow musicians.

Roamer McQueen is the cutest fat guy I ever met. He is a talented bassist and, from what I could gather, the heart and soul of the trio that gigged three days a week at Omega. He was extremely kind to me in those rushed, nerve-wracking days when I was rehearsing with him and Hank Thayer, the elegant pianist at the center of the group. In fact they were both wonderful to me.

For whatever reason, men seem compelled to come up with pet names for me. Roamer had dubbed me Big Legs. Canny showman that he was, he promised me a juicy solo for every low-cut blouse I wore to the gig. He is a riot.

I was subbing for sax player Gene Price, the third Musketeer, whose penchant for cheese grits and filterless cigarettes had him in the hospital for bypass surgery.

If I have to say so myself, I looked incredible in that button-up-the-back number I bought on Prince Street. Before I left the apartment that night, I asked Mama Lou and Dilsey (that is what I named the new doll) to work their special hoodoo to bring me good fortune at the gig. I blew each of them a kiss as I breezed out the door. I hopped right on the First Avenue bus, whistling "Liza" as most of the sentient males checked me out on the long seat at the back. I was riding pretty damn high.

Yeah. Once again I was making the mistake of not paying attention to another old black female figure in my life. Her name is Ernestine and—being my stern if quixotic conscience—she can be a real pain in the butt. Ernestine doesn't seem to like it very much when I'm riding high. I'm sure she was trying to warn me, but that night I just wasn't listening.

They fed us at the restaurant; that was part of the

deal. And the food wasn't bad. Certainly it was better than the pay. But in any case I was too keyed up to eat.

Both Aubrey and Justin were working that night and couldn't make the set, but they had promised to come see me later in the week.

I'd miss them, sure, but the one I found myself so looking forward to seeing was Ida Williams, the doll lady. It was almost like having your eccentric grandmother out there cheering for you on opening night.

I had gotten into the habit of dropping off containers of hot tea at her table every time I was in the vicinity of the farmers market. Sometimes Ida looked like the tough old bird and master salesperson I had first encountered, and sometimes she seemed frail as parchment, distracted and rueful. Complicated, in other words. I was hoping that someday soon I could talk my mom into coming into the city so that the three of us could go out to lunch.

I had been told that Omega did well. No lie, apparently: the ordinarily supercool maître d' was overwhelmed. People were pouring in. Drinks flowing. A good buzz in the room. Omega was a far cry from some smoky basement club where Monk and Charlie Rouse or Art Tatum or Max Roach was about to make history and (*your favorite junkie horn player's name here*) was out back scoring a nickel bag. But what the hell? This was still fun. I was still riding high.

The first set started at nine. Hank had a pretty arrangement of "Stella by Starlight" that was to open the set. The three of us stood schmoozing on the slightly raised platform near the front window of the restaurant.

In the midst of the throng of customers I spotted Ida talking to the coat check lady, who was helping her with her wrap.

Go on, Ida! Wow, what a dress. Classic chic-lady-out-cabareting threads. I wondered if she had found it in one of the expensive antique clothing stores in town, or if it was a number she'd been keeping in mothballs since the fifties. Understated nubby wool, clinging in all the right places, too. As Justin would say, not a sequin in sight. Plus, she had done her hair up in a fabulous finger wave.

I broke into a grin and waved hello, but she was too far away. She didn't see me. The small table near the bandstand was all arranged for her, and I was just about to step down to thank her for coming and find out what she wanted to drink. But that never happened.

The room suddenly exploded.

Gunfire and shrieks of terror.

Customers and staff alike went diving for the floor. I felt Hank's fingers around my wrist. He snatched me under the piano seat and my saxophone went bumping off the bandstand.

It was all over in a few seconds. There was confused disbelief on every face in the room: no, the sky wasn't falling; no, we weren't being robbed of our jewels by a band of masked brigands; no, the lunatic terrorists were not herding us into the back room. None of that.

Then what the fuck had just happened?

Roamer and Hank were on their feet again, brushing off their suits and exchanging confounded looks.

I remembered then. Ida!

I hoped she hadn't been trampled in all the confusion.

I ran to the maître d's station, where a knot of people were staring down at the floor in horror, all the women in the group with their hands at their mouths.

Ida.

One perfect hole in the middle of her face. A pool of bloody goo under her head.

I dropped to the floor and began a frantic check for any signs of life. Useless. I let out a dreadful deep moan that soon shot up into the high register. After that, I must've spaced out completely—gone somewhere deep in my own head. I went into some sort of trance and I didn't come out of it until I felt Roamer and Hank leading me to a chair.

"Oh no," I wailed, over and over. "Not again."

About the Author

CHARLOTTE CARTER worked as an editor and teacher and is a longtime fan of mystery fiction and film noir. She lives in New York.